Cyra

Hero

BY
EDMOND ROSTAND

A new adaptation by
ERNA KRUCKEMEYER

SAMUEL FRENCH, INC.
45 West 25th Street NEW YORK 10010
7623 Sunset Boulevard HOLLYWOOD 90046
LONDON TORONTO

Printed in U.S.A.

ISBN 0 573 60128 3

Following is a copy of the program of the original production of this version, at The Hughes High School, Cincinnati, March 8, 1934. This production was a collaboration of the Alumnal Players, and the Sages.

CAST

Cyrano de Bergerac	*Stanley Waxman '32*
Roxane	*Laurette Fillbrandt '32*
Christian de Neuvillette	*Al. Field*
Comte de Guiche	*Stanley Posthorn*
Ragueneau	*Edward Pandorf*
Le Bret	*William Saben*
Captain Carbon de Castel Jaloux	*Henry Merkel*
The Cadets of Gascony	*Randolph Peters* *Paul Seebohm* *Harold Wegman* *Laurence Bloom* *Lester Rupp* *Ramon Lindberg* *Edward Lang* *Wilbur Fitzgerald* *Theodore Batterson*
Lignere	*Franklin Rothenbush*
Vicomte de Valvert	*Tom Colter*
Richelieu	*Richard N. Kohl*
A Marquis	*Albert Weber*
Monfleury	*Lester Rupp*
Bellerose	*William Grimme*
Cuigy	*Dave Baker*
Brissaille	*Art Meinberg*
A Musketeer	*Edward Lang*
A Cutpurse	*Allan Moritz*
Bertrandou the Fifer	*Leo Simon*
A Capuchin	*Donald Braverman*
Duenna	*Helen Zimmermann*

CAST (*Continued*)

Orange Girl........................*Irene Wander*
Flower Girl......................*Alice Hambleton*
Mother Marguerite..................*Elma Wood*
Sister Marthe..................*Josephine Lerman*
Sister Claire.......................*Jane Lawson*
Ladies — *Margaret Anne Schmidt, Helen Derrick, Estelle Krolfifer, Genevieve Ihorst, Anne McLaughlin and Betty Franklin*
Actresses—*Rita Nauman, Jane Kyrk, Myrtle Williams, and Willa May Stock*

ACT I

A Performance at the Hotel Bourgogne, Paris—1640.

ACT II

A meeting at Ragueneau's Shop—morning of the next day.

ACT III

Roxane's Kiss—one night a few weeks later—under her balcony.

ACT IV

The Cadets of Gascony at the siege of Arras—at dawn a few weeks later.

ACT V

Cyrano's Gazette—in a Convent Garden one autumn day at dusk—fifteen years later.

PREFACE

Cyrano with his strange mixture of courage, independence and bravado is a character that appeals strongly to the high school boy and girl. In addition, the play itself offers an opportunity for the things every high school or college director is aiming to impress upon his students—simple and effective staging—a study of an important phase in the history of the drama—and what is most important in this day of sordid realism, the production of a play which is at the same time good theatre *and* good literature. Again—it offers a splendid stepping stone to Shakespeare.

The text of this version is an adaptation of the Richard Mansfield edition by Howard Thayer Kingsbury and the changes both in translation and arrangement were necessitated by the purpose for which this text is designed—*i. e.*, to secure for groups outside the commercial theatre an acting version that does not make impossible demands upon the producer both in respect to artistic staging and character portrayal, and at the same time retains the atmosphere of the period to which it belongs.

An effort has been made to make the plot move swiftly and clearly and yet preserve the poetry and romantic beauty of the original. All parts which make the play a difficult one to be handled by amateurs have been omitted. For example, because the difficult details of the pastry shop both in staging and characterization seem utterly beyond amateurs, ACT II becomes a room adjoining the shop and Ragueneau himself hardly more than a devoted admirer of Cyrano. Again—in order to cut the length of the play as a whole and still preserve its unity and sense of completeness some liberties were taken in translation. The balcony scene and the charming exposition of Cyrano's ways of reaching the moon are examples of this method. The present version was tried out at Hughes High School, Cincinnati, Ohio, in two evening performances on March 8 and 9, 1934, to capacity houses (sixteen hundred) and was received with enthusiasm by an audience made up, in addition to friends of the cast, of a large group of people well known in the artistic circles of this city.

NOTE ON THE MUSIC

The music used in this version and indicated in the text is from *A Cyrano Suite*, by Frederick Rosse.

ACT I

SCENE: *The Hall of the Hotel de Bourgogne, Paris, 1640. The curtain rises on a dark stage.* BELLEROSE *enters with lighted lantern.* FIRST CAVALIER *enters from auditorium* R.

(*LIGHT CUES—Blue and Red Footlights come up slightly.*)

BELLEROSE. Holloa! Your fifteen pence.

FIRST CAVALIER. [*Brushing past him*] I come in free.

BELLEROSE. Why?

FIRST CAVALIER. I'm a guardsman of the Royal Household.

BELLEROSE. [*To* SECOND CAVALIER *entering from auditorium* L.] And you?

SECOND CAVALIER. Oh, no!

BELLEROSE. But——

SECOND CAVALIER. [*Haughtily*] I'm a musketeer!

FIRST CAVALIER. [*To* SECOND CAVALIER, *pointing to play bill*]

The play does not begin till two o'clock.
The house is empty; let us try our foils.

SECOND CAVALIER. What is the play to-day? [*Looks at poster.*] Ah—" La Clorise."

[*They fence down* R. *A* GUARDSMAN *saunters in and is leaving when a* FLOWER GIRL *enters down* L. *They meet.*]

GUARD. Sweet of you to come while lights are low.

FIRST CAVALIER. [*Fencing*] A hit!

GUARD. [*To* GIRL] A kiss!

FLOWER GIRL. They'll see us.

[GUARD *laughs, puts his arm around her, and they walk up stage.*]

ORANGE GIRL. [*Enters, meets* FLOWER GIRL *and* GUARD, *and laughs*] Oranges, raspberry syrup, lemonade ——

THREE PAGES. [*Enter* R., *holding hands, singing and dancing*]

Tra la la la la la la la lere.

[BELLEROSE *orders them out. They pretend to obey, but hide on stairs.* ORANGE GIRL *approaches* CAVALIERS.]

ORANGE GIRL. Oranges, raspberry syrup, lemonade ——

[CAVALIERS *go to table for refreshments. A* MARQUIS *enters* R. PAGES *get busy with pea shooters.*]

MARQUIS. Lights—I say!

[BELLEROSE *rushes forward, bowing obsequiously to an irate gentleman.*]

FIRST CAVALIER. The Marquis.

SECOND CAVALIER. What! On the floor?

MARQUIS. How now? No lights?

I enter like a tradesman! Fie! No crowding?

No treading on the toes?

[*He glares at the embarrassed* BELLEROSE *and the amused* CAVALIERS. *Two more* NOBLES *enter.*]

Cuigy! Brissaille!

[*After kissing them French fashion, the* MARQUIS *turns on* BELLEROSE.]

You dolt! Lights!

[BELLEROSE *hurries off to do his bidding.*]

CUIGY. Here before the candles?

MARQUIS. [*Peevishly*] Shh—be still. You put me in a temper.

BRISSAILLE. Console yourself, Marquis. [*Pointing.*] Here comes the lamplighter.

(*Lights go up gradually to full.*)

[*Others now come in. The* LAMPLIGHTER *becomes the center of interest. A chandelier is lowered and the candles are lighted while the crowd gathers around, breaking into delighted exclamations as it is raised in place. The* PAGES *are in evidence with their pea shooters and a* PICKPOCKET *enters and looks around.* CADETS *enter with* THREE LADIES *who seat themselves in box* R. *Three other* LADIES *are escorted to box* L. BRISSAILLE *goes to box* L., *bows and converses.* CUIGY *and* MARQUIS *have same business* R. CHRISTIAN *and* LIGNIERE *enter, bow to ladies, look up at still empty box above door, then approach the other* NOBLEMEN. *They bow, except the* MARQUIS, *who simply stares.* LIGNIERE *is somewhat dishevelled, looks dissipated but distinguished.* CHRISTIAN *is very handsome and well dressed, although a bit behind the fashion.*]

CUIGY. Ligniere!

LIGNIERE. [*Bows, introducing*] Baron Christian de Neuvillette. Messieurs de Cuigy—[*looks toward* BRISSAILLE, *who joins them*] de Brissaille.

CUIGY and BRISSAILLE. Charmed.

LIGNIERE. He's just from Touraine.

CHRISTIAN. Yes, I have been
Scarce twenty days in Paris. But to-morrow
I join the Guards to serve with the Cadets.

ORANGE GIRL. Oranges—milk —— [*Smiling at* CHRISTIAN.]

FLOWER GIRL. [*From other side*] Flowers, Monsieur?

CHRISTIAN. Ah —— [*He selects a flower, refuses refreshments, but gives* ORANGE GIRL *a coin. She goes to* LIGNIERE.]

ORANGE GIRL. Oranges—milk ——? [*He waves her aside.*] Muscatel?

[*He looks interested, follows her to table, then changes his mind.* RAGUENEAU *enters. He is a little man, rather fat and beaming, dressed in the Sunday costume of a pastry cook. There are cries in the crowd as he enters.*]

LIGNIERE. [*To* CHRISTIAN] She is not here. I'm going.

CHRISTIAN. No—stay, I pray! She'll come.

BRISSAILLE. There's Ragueneau!

[RAGUENEAU *advances.*]

CROWD. Ragueneau!

CUIGY. The prince of pastry cooks.

BRISSAILLE. And friend of poets.

LIGNIERE. [*To* CHRISTIAN] Permit me to present good Ragueneau —— [*Looks around at all.*]

RAGUENEAU. [*Confused*]
You honor me too much. But gentlemen,
Has Monsieur Cyrano not yet arrived?
[*Looks around.*]
Astonishing!

LIGNIERE. But why?

RAGUENEAU. Montfleury plays.

LIGNIERE.

'Tis true, this barrel plays Phaeton to-night.
But what cares Cyrano?

RAGUENEAU. You do not know?
He hates Montfleury and has forbidden him
To appear upon the stage for a whole month.

LIGNIERE. Well, then ——

RAGUENEAU. Montfleury plays!

LIGNIERE. Well?

RAGUENEAU. That is what
I came to see.

CHRISTIAN. This Cyrano—who is he?

MARQUIS. Cyrano?

CUIGY. He's the Gascon with the sword. [*Laughs.*]

MARQUIS. Noble?

CUIGY. Quite! He's in the Guards. [LE BRET *approaches, bows, crosses to* RAGUENEAU.]
But—here—
His friend, Le Bret, can tell you. (*Bows.*) Ah, Le Bret,
You look for Bergerac?

LE BRET. Yes—and for trouble.

MARQUIS. He must be an extraordinary man!

LE BRET. He is. The choicest soul of mortal men.

[MARQUIS *stares through his monocle.*]

RAGUENEAU. A poet ——

CUIGY. Swordsman ——

MARQUIS. Indeed!

BRISSAILLE. Philosopher ——

LE BRET. Musician ——

LIGNIERE. And of such appearance, too.

RAGUENEAU.

One of those wild swashbucklers in a mask.
Hat with three plumes and doublet with six points.
His cloak behind falls over his long sword
Like the tail of a strutting chanticleer.
Prouder far than all the Artabans
Of Gascony. A punchinello figure
With a nose—what a nose! You gaze—
And then you gaze again, and cry, "But no!
It cannot be. It is exaggerated."
Then you smile, and to yourself you say,
"Presently he'll take it off." Alas,—
That Monsieur de Bergerac will never do.

LE BRET.

He keeps it—and Heaven help the man
Who looks at it askance.

MARQUIS. Really?

LE BRET. [*Sharply*] Yes.

RAGUENEAU. His sword's the half of the dread shears of Fate ——

(*MUSIC CUES—Roxane Theme softly.*)
(*LIGHT CUES—Bring up spot on box.*)

MARQUIS. Indeed! [*Then, seeing* ROXANE *enter the box with her duenna*]

Oh, I say—gentlemen—behold;
Is she not frightfully ravishing?
Her cheek is delicate as the blossoming peach,
Her strawberry lips ripe red and smiling
Warm us with love for her.

CUIGY. But her cold glance
Strikes chill into our hearts—the chill of death.

[*All turn and bow to* ROXANE, *who responds graciously.*]

CHRISTIAN. [*Noticing the commotion, looks up*] 'Tis she! [*To* LIGNIERE.] There—quick—up there in the box—her name?

LIGNIERE.

Madeleine Robin, but—called Roxane—
A beauty and an intellectual.

CHRISTIAN. Alas!

LIGNIERE. Unmarried—orphan—and a cousin
Of Cyrano of whom we spoke.

[*Two gentlemen, one very distinguished looking, enter the box and talk to* ROXANE.]

CHRISTIAN. [*Starting*] This man ——?

LIGNIERE. [*Mischievously*]

Ha-ha. The Comte de Guiche—in love with her—
Married to Richelieu's niece—would marry Roxane
To him [*indicates other man*]—his gloomy friend —Vicomte Valvert,
Old and dull and—well—obliging ——

CHRISTIAN. [*In a rage*] Hein?

LIGNIERE.

She's not consented—but de Guiche has power.
He well can persecute a simple girl—
And he is not above such persecution.

CHRISTIAN. Sacre!

LIGNIERE. [*Smoothly*]

I have written a little song—
A naughty little song about this game—
A naughty little game—n'est-ce pas, my friend?
Shall I sing it?

CHRISTIAN. No. Good-night. [*Crosses behind* LIGNIERE.]

LIGNIERE. [*Stopping him*] You go?

CHRISTIAN. To Valvert—first ——

LIGNIERE. You'd better have a care—
The man's a swordsman. Wait! She noticed you!

(*Music stops.*)

CHRISTIAN. [*Spellbound*] Roxane!

LIGNIERE. I might as well be leaving. Good day.

[CHRISTIAN *is unconscious of him. He shrugs and leaves.* LE BRET *and* RAGUENEAU *cross down* R.]

LE BRET. [*To* RAGUENEAU] No sign of Cyrano?

RAGUENEAU. Wait and see.

LE BRET. Why does he hate Montfleury so?

RAGUENEAU. Why?
That's plain! Monsieur de Bergerac's a poet ——

[BELLEROSE *comes in to light the footlights.*]

CROWD. [*Murmuring anxiously for the play to begin*] The play!—Footlights! etc.

[*The* PAGES *are busy with their pea shooters.* DE GUICHE *and* VALVERT *come down from the box. The crowd make way for them. The* MARQUIS *follows in their wake.* CHRISTIAN *stands gazing at them in rage when the* PICKPOCKET *approaches him.*]

DE GUICHE. I go upon the stage. You'll come, Valvert?

CHRISTIAN. Valvert! I'll throw my glove into his face!
[*He reaches into his pocket and encounters the hand of the pickpocket who has taken the opportunity during* CHRISTIAN'S *abstraction.*]

PICKPOCKET. Oh!

CHRISTIAN. I want a glove.

PICKPOCKET. And find a hand.
Let go—I'll tell a secret ——

CHRISTIAN. What?

PICKPOCKET. Ligniere—
That friend of yours who left, is good as dead.
He wrote a song—about the great—and so
A hundred men—I'm one—to-night are posted ——

CHRISTIAN. A hundred? And by whom?

PICKPOCKET. A secret ——

CHRISTIAN. Oh.

PICKPOCKET. Among professionals.

CHRISTIAN. Where will they be?

PICKPOCKET. The Port de Nesle—on his way home to-night ——

CHRISTIAN.
What swine! I'll tell him. [PICKPOCKET *nods.*]
But—Roxane!—
Leave her
Here with them? And yet—Ligniere—I'll go.

[*He hurries out. The* MARQUIS *struts over to* DE GUICHE *and* VALVERT *on the stage and bows, but they merely ogle him. The audience settles down.* LE BRET *and* RAGUENEAU *take rather conspicuous places. The mischievous boys make the most of the situation.* RAGUENEAU *and* LE BRET *cross and sit at table.*]

LE BRET. Montfleury opens the play.
RAGUENEAU. And no de Bergerac.
LE BRET. So much the better.

[MONTFLEURY *appears, very fat, in the costume of a shepherd, his hat decorated with roses and cocked over his ear. He is blowing upon a pipe ornamented with ribbons.*]

FIRST CAVALIER. Montfleury!
CROWD. Brave Montfleury!
MONTFLEURY. Thrice happy he ——
VOICE. [*From door slightly ajar*] Wretch, was't not for a month I warned you off?

[*Everyone turns round and murmurs, "What is it?" People stand up in boxes to look.*]

CUIGY. Cyrano.
LE BRET. Himself.
RAGUENEAU. [*Joyfully*] Monsieur de Bergerac.
CYRANO. King of clowns—leave the stage at once.
CROWD. Oh—why—etc.
MONTFLEURY. Now—now ——
CYRANO. You do not instantly obey me?
CROWD. Proceed, Montfleury ——
CYRANO. Well—well—monarch of mountebanks,
Must I plant a forest on your shoulders?
[*He shakes his cane at him. Just the top of the cane is visible above the crowd.*]
MONTFLEURY. [*Weakening*] Thrice happy ——
CYRARNO. [*Gets up on chair*] Go! [CROWD *falls back and* CYRANO *stands with folded arms, his hat cocked, his mustache bristling and his nose terrible. A little boy places himself near* CYRANO *and looks*

up at him with curiosity and delight.] Presently I shall grow angry.

MONTFLEURY. [*Weakly*] Messieurs, you will protect me?

DE GUICHE. Proceed.

MONTFLEURY. [*Making another attempt*] Thrice ——

CYRANO.

Good! I approach the stage as 'twere a side-board,
To carve in slices this Italian sausage.
[*Turning back his cuffs.*]

MARQUIS. [*Crossing in front of* CYRANO *and staring at him*] Who might you be—Samson?

CYRANO. Precisely.

And will you kindly lend me, sir, your jawbone?
[*Laughs, catcalls, etc., i. e., "Woof! Baah! Cockadoo! Meow!" Business of* PAGES *with their pea shooters.*]
Silence—all!

CROWD. Meow—woof—baah ——

CYRANO.

I order you straightway to hold your tongues.
I send a general challenge to you all!
Come—each in turn—I'll give to each his number;
Come, who is the man who bravely heads the list?
You, sir? No! You, sir? No!—Once more—
Let all who wish to die now raise their hands.
No hand? No name?—'Tis well—I shall go on.

[CROWD *murmurs.*]

MONTFLEURY. I—really ——

CYRANO.
Silence! Three times I'll clap my hands, full moon—
You'll vanish at the third. [*Sits down comfortably.*]
One—
[CROWD *murmurs.* PAGE *aims pea shooter at* MONTFLEURY.]
Two ——

MONTFLEURY. Perhaps I'd better ——

CYRANO. Three!

[MONTFLEURY *disappears.*]

CROWD. Coward—come back—etc.

MARQUIS.
Monsieur de—ah—ah—pray, what grounds
Have you for hating—Montfleury?

CYRANO.
Two—
And each alone is quite enough.—First,
He is a wretched actor who mouths the lines
That ought to soar on their own wings—second—
That is my secret.

FIRST LADY. [*Enraged*] But you rob us of "Clorise" by Baro.

CYRANO. Baro—bah!

SECOND LADY. Our Baro.

THIRD LADY. Did you hear that?

FIRST LADY. Mon dieu—it is preposterous—really.

CYRANO. [*Turning to the boxes, gallantly*]
Fair creatures, shine upon us, blossom as
The flowers in our gardens, charm, or be
As music soft that's heard in dreams—inspire—

Enchant with smiles, but do not try—I pray—
To criticize.

BELLEROSE. [*Steps out on stage, accompanied by* ACTRESSES *and* MONTFLEURY, *who keeps in background*] The money must be returned.

CYRANO.
Ah, Bellerose—that is a word of sense.
Here, catch.

[*He throws his purse to* BELLEROSE *who examines it delightedly and is surrounded by* ACTRESSES. CROWD *murmurs approvingly.*]

BELLEROSE. For this price, sir, I give you leave
To come each night to stop Clorise.

[*One* ACTRESS *throws a kiss to* CYRANO, *another puts out hand to* BELLEROSE *for money, a third embraces* MONTFLEURY.]

CROWD. Hoo!—Hoo!

BELLEROSE. Clear the hall!

[*The* CROWD *begin to move and* CYRANO *looks pleased.* DE GUICHE *and* VALVERT *come down from the stage.*]

DE GUICHE. This fellow grows tiresome. Will no one answer him?

VALVERT. Observe—I will put him in his place. [*Takes his stand before* CYRANO.] Ah—hem—your nose—your nose is rather large!

CYRANO. [*Gravely*] Rather.

VALVERT. Oh—well —— [*Simpers.*]

CYRANO. [*Coolly*] That is all?

[VALVERT *merely shrugs.*]

'Tis not enough!
You might have said a multitude of things,

As for example thus: aggressively:—
Sir—had I such a nose, I'd cut it off.
Friendly:—How do you drink with such a nose?
You ought to have a mediæval goblet
Made for it. Descriptive:—Is it a crag?
A peak? A cape? But nay—did I say cape?
It is, it seems, more like a peninsula.
Inquisitive:—A scissors case, perchance?
Or a portfolio?—Or, graciously:—
I see that you are fond of little birds—
You give them this to rest their little feet.
Or, insolently:—No—you do not dare
To smoke—your neighbors would cry out, "Behold,
The chimney is afire." Warning:—Careful,
This weight will drag you down.—Or thoughtfully:—
These delicate colors fade out so in the sun.
Pedantic:—Beast of Aristophanes!
Hippacamelephantocamelos!
Dramatic:—When it bleeds, it is the Red Sea.
Admiring:—What a sign for a perfumer.
Poetic:—A triton? This thy couch? Naive:—
This monument is interesting; what are
The visiting hours? Rustic:—Hey, what? You call
That there a nose? Na—na—that is a turnip—
A prize turnip—or a dwarf melon—what?
You bantling,—these, then, are the things you might
Have said—had you some learning or some wit;
But wit and learning—most forlorn of beings,
You've never had an atom; and as for letters,
You only have the four that spell out "Fool!"

Moreover, had you the invention here
Before this noble gathering, to assail
Me with these pleasantries—as I have done—
You would not even have pronounced the quarter
Of the half of the beginning;—for I
Myself say them about myself with dash
Enough, but I suffer no one else even
To whisper them.

DE GUICHE. Vicomte—leave off—enough ——

VALVERT. [*Choking*]
These arrogant grand airs! The fellow is
A boor—who—look at him—not even gloves!
No lace—no buckles on his shoes, and not
A single ribbon!

CYRANO. [*Quietly*]
My furbelows are of the soul: my graces
Of the mind and heart. I do not deck
Me like a popinjay to sally forth
With insults not yet wiped away: nor yet
With conscience sallow—sleep still in its eyes,
Honor in rags—and scruples in deep mourning:
I am—in short—not the mere semblance of
A man, but yet his soul, clad, as it were
In shining armor—bearing on my crest
My plume of freedom—white, unstained, erect:
For ribbons, I have daring deeds. I twirl
My wit as my mustache, and as I pass
Among the crowds in this old town of ours,
I make bold truth ring out like spurs.

VALVERT. But, sir—

CYRANO.
No gloves? A pity, too. I had one left—
One—of a worn out pair, which troubled me;
I left it recently—in someone's face.

VALVERT.

Knave, rascal, booby, flatfoot, scum o' the earth ——

CYRANO. [*Taking off his hat as if* VALVERT *had just introduced himself*] Ah?—and I—Cyrano Savinien—Hercule de Bergerac ——

[*Laughter from the crowd.*]

VALVERT. [*In a rage*] Buffoon!

CYRANO. [*Crying as if in sudden pain*] Oh ——

VALVERT. [*To* DE GUICHE] What is he saying now?

CYRANO. My sword blade tingles ——

VALVERT. Come on then. [*Draws sword.*]

CYRANO. I'll strike you charmingly ——

VALVERT. Poet ——

CYRANO.

Ah! And while I fence, I'll improvise
For you—a bit—say, a ballade.

VALVERT. Ballade?

CYRANO. A poem of three stanzas and eight lines ——

VALVERT. Oh ——

CYRANO. And a refrain of four ——

VALVERT. You!

CYRANO.

And as I improvise, we'll fence. And then
With the last line of the refrain—I'll thrust
And touch you, sir.

VALVERT. No ——

CYRANO. No?—The Ballade
Of Monsieur de Bergerac's duel with a booby.

VALVERT. Hein?

CYRANO. Merely the title!

CROWD. [*Excited*] In line! A duel!

[*Tableau:—A circle of interested onlookers*—PAGES *on*

shoulders of people, women standing in boxes. R., DE GUICHE *and* VALVERT; L., LE BRET, RAGUENEAU, CUIGY, *etc.*]

CYRANO. [*Closing his eyes for a moment.*]
Wait—let me choose my rhymes.—I have them now.—
My hat I toss lightly away;
From my shoulders I slowly let fall
The cloak which conceals my array,
And my sword from my scabbard I call.
Like Celadon, graceful and tall,
Like Scaramouche—quick hand and brain—
And I warn you, my friend, once for all,
I shall thrust when I end the refrain!
[*Salutes. Swords meet.*]

You were rash thus to join in the fray:
Like a fowl I shall carve you up small,
Your ribs 'neath your doublet so gay,
Your breast where the blue ribbons fall,
Ding, dong! ring your bright trappings all:
My point flits like a fly on the pane
As I clearly announce to the hall
I shall thrust when I end the refrain!

I need one more rhyme for "array"—
You give ground, you turn white as the wall—
And so lend me the word, "runaway"—
There, you have let your point fall
As I parry your best lunge of all;—
I begin a new line:—the end's plain,
Your skewer hold tight, lest it fall;
I shall thrust when I end the refrain!
[*Then solemnly.*]

Prince, on the Lord you must call!
I gain ground, I advance once again;
I feint, I lunge [*lunging*]—there! That is all!
[VALVERT *falls;*—CYRANO *staggers*—CROWD *cries out, then is quiet.*]
For I thrust as I end the refrain!

(CYRANO *Theme.*)

[*Shouts of applause. Flowers and handkerchiefs are thrown down.* OFFICERS *surround* CYRANO *to congratulate him.* RAGUENEAU *dances with enthusiasm.* LE BRET *is overjoyed.* VALVERT'S *friends lift him and lead him away.* CYRANO *bows to ladies as they come up from* R., *then* L.]

CROWD. Oh!—Ah!
GUARD. Superb!
FIRST LADY. A pretty stroke!
RAGUENEAU. Magnificent!
LE BRET. Mad folly!
CROWD. Compliments—
Congratulations—Bravo ——
SECOND LADY. He's a hero!

[RAGUENEAU *calls* CYRANO'S *attention to* ROXANE, *who is leaning over balcony. He turns and bows. She throws a flower.*]

(*Music stops.*)

MUSKETEER. [*Advances and shakes* CYRANO'S *hand*]
Will you allow me, sir, to say, "Well done"?
For these are things I understand. Superb,
Monsieur de Bergerac.
[*He goes out quickly, while all gaze at him.*]
CYRANO. That gentleman is ——?

LE BRET. D'Artagnan —— [*Taking* CYRANO's *arm.*] Come, let us talk.

CYRANO. Let the crowds go out first. [*To* BELLEROSE.] May I wait?

BELLEROSE. [*With great respect*]
Certainly, Monsieur de Bergerac.
Strike—close the house! Leave the lights.
We shall return to rehearse to-morrow's farce.
[CROWDS *go out slowly.* BELLEROSE *bows elaborately to* CYRANO.]
You do not dine?

CYRANO. I? No ——

LE BRET. Because ——?

CYRANO. Because—
[*Changes his tone as* BELLEROSE *leaves.*]
I have no money.

LE BRET. But the purse of gold ——

CYRANO. [*Laughs*] Farewell, paternal pension!

LE BRET. You've given all?
Until next month you've ——

CYRANO. Nothing.

LE BRET. What folly!

CYRANO. But what a gesture.

ORANGE GIRL. [*Coming down from sideboard*]
Hein? Pardon, Monsieur;
To see you hungry breaks my heart. See?
Here is everything. Take what you wish.

CYRANO. [*Taking off his hat*]
My Gascon pride forbids, my child, to take
One dainty from your hands; and yet, since this,
I fear, would cause you pain, I shall accept ——
[*Goes to sideboard.*]
Oh—nothing much—a grape.
[*She gives him a bunch of grapes.*]

No! But one;
This glass of water—[*she starts to pour wine*] clear!

ORANGE GIRL. But please, Monsieur,
A little wine?

CYRANO. [*Refusing*] And half a macaroon! [*He returns the other half.*]

LE BRET. But this is foolish!

ORANGE GIRL. Please, not something more? [*She crosses in front of table.*]

CYRANO. Why, yes, your hand to kiss, my child.

LE BRET. H'm ——

ORANGE GIRL. Thank you, Monsieur. [*Curtseys.*] Good-night. [*She goes out.*]

CYRANO. [*To* LE BRET] Talk;—I will listen. [*He takes his place before the sideboard and arranges his dinner.*] Dinner. [*Eats macaroon.*] Drink. [*Drinks water.*] Dessert. [*Takes grape.*] Lord, I was hungry. [*Sits down comfortably.*]

LE BRET.
My friend, these boobies with their grandiose airs
Will ruin you if you consort with them.
Talk to men of sense and get from them
The effect of this mad sally. The Cardinal ——

CYRANO. [*Interested*] The Cardinal was there?

LE BRET. [*Paying no attention*] Must have esteemed it ——

CYRANO. Quite original.

LE BRET. Perhaps—and yet ——

CYRANO.
He is a poet and will no doubt rejoice
That we have closed a fellow poet's play.

LE BRET. You make too many enemies, my friend.

CYRANO. About how many have I made to-night?

LE BRET. Without the women—forty-eight.

CYRANO. Come, count.

LE BRET. Montfleury and the Academy; de Guiche, Valvert ——

CYRANO. Enough —— You make me happy.

LE BRET.

So be it! But come—the reason why you hate
Montfleury? [CYRANO *hesitates.*]—The truth!

CYRANO. I hate him ——

LE BRET. Yes, but why?

CYRANO.

I hate him ever since one night he dared
To smile on —— Oh, my friend, I seemed to see
Upon a flower fair, a great snail crawling ——

LE BRET. What? And can it be ——?

CYRANO. [*With a bitter smile*] That I should love? [*Then seriously.*] I love.

LE BRET. And may I know? You never told me ——

CYRANO.

Whom I love? Think —— It is forbidden me
To dream of love from e'en the most ill favored;
Yet—bah! I, with this nose which goes before me
Half a mile—whom should I love but her
Who is the fairest in the whole wide world.

LE BRET. The fairest ——

CYRANO. [*Nods*]

Most brilliant and most delicate.
[*Dejectedly.*]
The fairest hair ——

LE BRET. Mon dieu, who is this woman?

CYRANO.

He who knows her smile knows perfect bliss.
Not Venus in her iridescent shell,

Nor Dian in green, leafy woods, is so
Divine as she, when, in her chair, she's borne
Through these old Paris streets.

LE BRET. [*Nods*] It is quite clear!

CYRANO. Transparent—yes.

LE BRET. Your cousin, Madeleine——

CYRANO. [*Nods*] Roxane.

LE BRET. Why not? Tell her that you love her.
You won great glory in her eyes to-day.

CYRANO.
Look at me, old friend, and tell what hope
Remains for me with this protuberance.
Oh—I have no more illusions. Sometimes,
'Tis true, I sit alone in the blue dusk
Of evening, in a garden sweet with flowers;
My poor big devil of a nose inhales the Spring—
And I watch a boy and girl stroll arm in arm
Through the silvery light. Then I grow pensive,
And wish somehow I had a sweetheart, too,
To take my arm and walk with tiny steps
Beside me in the fragrant moonlit garden.
I dream and I forget;—when suddenly—
Bah—I see the shadow of my profile
On the garden wall!

LE BRET. [*With deep feeling*] My friend!

CYRANO. [*Nods*] Yes—
I have my hours of gloom, Le Bret, and oft
When quite alone——

LE BRET. You weep?

CYRANO. Ah—never that!
No—that would be too ugly—if a tear—
Than which there's nothing more sublime on earth—

Should trickle down this monstrous nose of mine—
I would not ridicule the loveliness
Of tears.

LE BRET.
But your wit—your courage. Why, this child
Who offered you just now this modest meal,
Did not — you plainly saw — avoid you. Come ——

CYRANO. That is the truth ——

LE BRET. Well, then, Roxane herself
Grew pale watching your duel.

CYRANO. She grew pale?

LE BRET.
'Twas clear that she was moved. Courage, man—
Speak to her!

[DUENNA *is admitted by* BELLEROSE.]

CYRANO. My nose—she'll laugh—and that
Is the only thing in this whole world I fear.

BELLEROSE. Monsieur—someone is asking for you.

CYRANO. Heavens!
Her Duenna ——

DUENNA. Someone wishes—in secret—
To see her cousin—who fought so valiantly.

CYRANO. See me?

DUENNA. See you. Someone has things to tell you.

CYRANO. Things—to tell me?

DUENNA. [*Mysteriously*] Things, Monsieur.

CYRANO. Mon dieu!

DUENNA. To-morrow at the blush of dawn
Someone will go to early mass.

CYRANO. Mon dieu!

DUENNA. And after that, where can one stop—and talk?

CYRANO. Where?

DUENNA. [*Nods*] In secret?—Well ——?

CYRANO. I'm thinking ——

DUENNA. Where?

CYRANO. Why—at Ragueneau the pastry cook's.

DUENNA. And that is ——

CYRANO. That is—oh—on the Rue St. Honore.

DUENNA. At seven o'clock. You will be there?

CYRANO. I will. [*The* DUENNA *bows low and exits.* CYRANO *falls over into* LE BRET'S *arms.* ACTRESSES *begin coming out to rehearse the play.*] From her—for me—a meeting.

LE BRET. You are sad
No more?

CYRANO. At least she knows that I exist.

LE BRET. And now—you will be calm?

[ACTRESSES *watch amusedly from stage.*]

CYRANO. Calm? Man,
I burn—I am a fire—I am a storm.
I want a regiment to put to rout.
I have ten hearts—a hundred arms, my friend—
'Tis not enough for me to hew down *dwarfs*,
Give me *giants!* [*He shouts at the top of his voice.*]

BELLEROSE. [*From stage*] Down there—quiet.

CYRANO. We go.

[*He starts to withdraw when* CUIGY, BRISSAILLE, *etc., come in with* LIGNIERE, L. *They are excited and* LIGNIERE *is very much frightened.*]

CUIGY. Cyrano—Ligniere has need of you ——

LIGNIERE. [*Showing crumpled letter*]
This letter says a hundred men will wait
For me to-night—because I wrote a song—
A little song. Let me go home with you
And sleep beneath your roof? A hundred men—
To-night—at the Port de Nesle.

CYRANO. A hundred? Good!
And you shall sleep at home.
[BELLEROSE *comes down with a lantern and regards the scene curiously.*]
Take that lantern.
I'll see you to your home.—A hundred men!
The rest may come with us—as audience.
But, gentlemen, remember now, no rescue—
Give me no help—whatever be the danger.

LE BRET. A hundred against one!

CYRANO. Oh, come, Le Bret,
Don't grumble.

LE BRET. But, 'tis madness!—One against
A hundred ——

CYRANO. Yes—to-night I fight a hundred.

ACTRESS. But why—one man against a hundred, pray?

CYRANO. Because they know this one man is my friend.

SECOND ACTRESS. I am going to see this fight.

THIRD ACTRESS. And I!

[*They go to the stage and pick up scarfs.* CADETS *and* CROWD *take the footlight candles.*]

(*Lights gradually dimmed.*)

CYRANO.
Come, all you madcap throng, your presence gay
Shall be Italian farce to Spanish drama—
Tiny tinkling bells to roll of drums.

CROWD. Bravo—My cloak—My cape—My lantern ——

[CADETS *offer arms to* ACTRESSES.]

(*Lights continue dimming.*)

CYRANO. Ready—
Now, violins, you'll play a tune for us.
Bravo! Women in costume—officers—
And twenty paces to the front [*takes his place*] —myself,
Alone, beneath the plume by glory placed.
'Tis understood—no one to lend a hand.
[*He swings the others into action as he speaks. He springs on to the stage.*]

(*Blue floods on back drop.*)

Ready—one—two—three. Bellerose, the door!
[BELLEROSE *opens wide the doors; moonlight streams in.* CYRANO *takes his place in the door. There is a sudden silence.*]
Paris sleeps, and through the silvery haze
The moonlight falls upon her peaked roofs,
And yonder, far beneath the misty veil
Shimmers the Seine—like a mysterious
And magic mirror. Ah—and you shall see
What you shall see. To the Port de Nesle!
(CYRANO *Theme.*)

[*He marches out and the procession follows to the music and shouting of " To the Port de Nesle! "*]

CURTAIN

ACT II

SCENE: *A room off from* RAGUENEAU'S *shop. Small tables and chairs, perhaps a sideboard.* RAGUENEAU *is dusting tables and arranging chairs, stopping now and then to gesticulate, as if engaged in a fencing match and accompanying his action with the words:*

(Lights up full.)

RAGUENEAU. I shall thrust when I end the refrain.

[CYRANO *enters suddenly. He seems excited.*]

CYRANO. What time is it?
RAGUENEAU. [*Looking at clock*] Six o'clock.
CYRANO. [*With a sigh*] An hour!
RAGUENEAU. It was splendid. I saw it all.
CYRANO. Hein?
RAGUENEAU. Your fight!
CYRANO. Which one?
RAGUENEAU. At the Hotel Burgogne—
The one ——
CYRANO. [*Intercepting disdainfully*] Ah, that!
RAGUENEAU. The duel fought in verse. [*Again he thrusts with an imaginary sword.*]
CYRANO. What time is it?
RAGUENEAU. [*Stops for a moment to look at the clock*]
Five minutes after six.
A ballade.—To think of writing one ——
[*Notices* CYRANO'S *wound.*]
—My friend,
You've hurt your hand!

CYRANO. A scratch—that's all!—But—
I'm expecting—ah—[*stammers*] could we—
could we—[RAGUENEAU *stares*]
Be alone?

RAGUENEAU. We ——?

CYRANO. Yes, I said it—we.

RAGUENEAU. A lady, Monsieur?

CYRANO. Why not?

RAGUENEAU. But here, Monsieur?

CYRANO. [*Frowning*] Here; where else is there for me to go?

RAGUENEAU. Ah—but ——

CYRANO. [*Roughly*] What time is it?

RAGUENEAU. Ten after six.

CYRANO. A pen! [*Seats himself and begins drumming nervously.*]

[RAGUENEAU *hurries away and comes back with paper, takes a quill from behind his ear and offers it to* CYRANO.]

RAGUENEAU. A swan's quill! [*He peers over* CYRANO'S *shoulder.* CYRANO *looks up, frowns;* RAGUENEAU *departs, confused, bowing.* CYRANO *bends himself to his task.*]

(ROXANE *Theme.*)

CYRANO. Roxane — Roxane — my love —— [*He writes, looks up as for inspiration—smiles, sighs—writes again.*]

[*During this there should be soft music. Two women are seen to pass by the window. They knock and* RAGUENEAU *admits them. One is young and beautiful and is masked; the other is middle-aged.*]

ROXANE. There he is.

[DUENNA *stares—nods and coughs.*]

CYRANO. [*Looks up, rises, upsets something*] Ah—Roxane—welcome! [*He makes an elaborate bow, and, taking* ROXANE's *hand to kiss, is about to lead her to a chair. He stares uncertainly at the* DUENNA, *sees* RAGUENEAU, *exchanges glances with* ROXANE, *beckons to* RAGUENEAU *who advances with a tray of pastry.*] Ah—are you fond of sweets?

[*The* DUENNA *has sat down as if prepared to stay.*]

DUENNA. [*Eagerly*] Oh, yes, Monsieur.
CYRANO. Then here's—a plate ——
DUENNA. Pooh ——
CYRANO. Which I shall fill—
With wine cakes? [*Holds up one and questions.*]
DUENNA. Please, Monsieur.
CYRANO. And cream puffs, too?
DUENNA. I dote on them.
CYRANO. [*Counts out cakes*] One, two, three, four, five, six.
DUENNA. Ah!
CYRANO. And tarts—fresh tarts with jam—hein?
You like them, too?
DUENNA. I dream of them at night! [*Takes plate eagerly.*]
CYRANO. Then please be kind enough to eat—elsewhere.
DUENNA. [*Nonplussed*] But ——
RAGUENEAU. I will find a place for her. [*Holds out his arm.*]
DUENNA. [*Delighted, goes with him, smiling, eating her cakes*] Monsieur!

[CYRANO *approaches* ROXANE *and helps take off her long coat.*]

CYRANO.

Mademoiselle, blessed be forevermore
This hour among all hours when you remembered—
So graciously remembered me and came
To tell me—ah, Mademoiselle—to tell ——

ROXANE.

To thank you first because the knavish dolt
Whom you put to the laugh with your good sword
Is he whom a great lord—in love with me ——

CYRANO. [*Quickly*] De Guiche?

ROXANE. [*Dropping her eyes*]
Has tried to force upon me as
A husband.

CYRANO. Then I have fought—and better so—
For your bright eyes—not for my ugly nose.

ROXANE. [*Looks at him under her lashes, nods faintly and goes toward the table.* CYRANO *places her chair. As she sits, she speaks*] Before I can confess to that ——

CYRANO. Yes ——? [*He comes around and takes his position on the table.*]

ROXANE.

I must find in you once more the comrade
Of my childhood; you with whom I played
In the old garden by the lake:—Remember?

CYRANO. [*Nods*] Every summer you came to Bergerac ——

ROXANE. The reeds then furnished wooden swords for you ——

CYRANO. And the corn, golden hair to deck your dolls.

ROXANE. It was a happy time!

CYRANO. Those sour blackberries!

ROXANE. [*Laughs*] At that time you did everything I asked you!

CYRANO. Roxane, in short skirts—was known as Madeleine.

ROXANE. Was I pretty then?

CYRANO. Not so bad ——

ROXANE.

Sometimes when you had cut your hand in climbing,
You ran to me: then I would play the mother
And say with voice that tried hard to be stern,
[*Takes his hand.*]
"What is this scratch, now?" [*Stops in surprise.*] Ah! Too bad!
And this?
[CYRANO *tries to draw back his hand.*]
No, show it to me! What:—at your age, still?
How came it?

CYRANO. Playing at the Port de Nesle.

[*She draws him over to chair at table and dips her handkerchief in a glass of water.* CYRANO *sits down.*]

Like a fond and happy little mother.

ROXANE.

Tell me, while I wash away the blood,
How many were there?

CYRANO. Oh, not quite a hundred.

ROXANE. Tell me ——

CYRANO. Oh—what does it matter? Rather
Tell me what you said you didn't dare ——

ROXANE.

I do dare now. The past with its sweet perfume
Gives me courage. Yes—I dare. Well, then—
I love someone ——

CYRANO. Ah!—

ROXANE. He doesn't know ——

CYRANO. Ah!—

ROXANE. At least not yet ——

CYRANO. Ah!

ROXANE. But soon will know ——

CYRANO. Ah!

ROXANE.

A poor lad who has loved me until now
Timidly, from afar, nor dared to speak.

CYRANO. Ah! [*Withdrawing his hand.*]

ROXANE.

No, leave your hand. It is all feverish—
But I have seen love trembling on his lips.

CYRANO. Ah!

ROXANE. [*Finishing the bandage made of her handkerchief*]

And do you know, my cousin, it is a fact—
He now is serving in your regiment.

CYRANO. Ah!

ROXANE. In your own company he's a cadet!

CYRANO. Ah! [*He leans way over eagerly and takes her hand.*]

ROXANE.

His forehead bears the stamp of wit—of genius.
He is proud — noble — young — brave — handsome ——

CYRANO. [*Starting, withdraws his hand quickly*] Handsome? [*He looks at her, then turns quickly away to hide his face.*]

ROXANE. Why—what's the matter?

CYRANO. With me?—Nothing.
It is—ah—my hand. It smarts a little.

ROXANE.
In short, I love him. I must tell you, too—
That I have seen him only at the play.

CYRANO. [*Still at a distance*] Then you have spoken ——

ROXANE. Only with our eyes.

CYRANO. But then—how can you know?

ROXANE. [*Shrugs*] People talk—
One hears—I know.

CYRANO. He's a cadet, you say?

ROXANE. Yes—in the guards.

CYRANO. His name ——?

ROXANE. De Neuvillette—
Baron Christian de Neuvillette.

CYRANO. The guards?
De Neuvillette?—He's not with us ——

ROXANE. But yes—
This morning, with Captain Castel-Jaloux.

CYRANO. Ah, how quickly do we lose our hearts!
[*He starts toward her.*]
But my poor child ——

DUENNA. Monsieur de Bergerac,
I've eaten all the cakes.

CYRANO. [*Impatiently*] Then go again—
And think how good they were.
[*She seems bewildered, but he looks at her commandingly and she withdraws. He turns to* ROXANE.]
But, my poor child,
You who love keen wit and courtly speech,
What if he be a man unlearned—a fool?

ROXANE. [*Shaking her head*] His hair is like a hero's from Durfé ——

CYRANO. But his mind?

ROXANE. Every word is brilliant.

CYRANO.
And yet you've spoken only with your eyes.
What if he be a blockhead?

ROXANE. Then I shall die.

CYRANO. [*Again walking away from her*]
And you have brought me here to tell me this?
I scarcely understand, Madame.

ROXANE. —But—
You've always been my brother—my big brother,
Have you not? And all your company
Are Gascons—are they not? Every one?
Quick to quarrel and perhaps to fight
With one who is no Gascon?

CYRANO. Yes—of course ——

ROXANE. Think how I tremble for him.

CYRANO. [*Emphatically*] With good reason.

ROXANE.
I thought of you. You were so brave, so strong—
Standing alone against a hundred ruffians ——
[*She puts her arm around his neck.*]

CYRANO. [*Struggling from her embrace*] 'Tis well. I will protect your little baron.

ROXANE.
You will? You really will protect him for me?
I've always had a warm friendship for you.

CYRANO. Yes, yes.

ROXANE. You'll be his friend?

CYRANO. I'll be his friend.

ROXANE. And he shall fight no duels?

CYRANO. [*Lifelessly*] On my oath.

ROXANE.

I am so fond of you!—Now I must go.

[*She quickly puts on her mask and a bit of lace over her head and speaks absent-mindedly.*]

But you have not yet told me of last night!
A hundred men! Dear cousin, what a feat!
Tell him to write. [*Throws him a kiss.*] I am so fond of you.

CYRANO. Yes, yes.

ROXANE. A hundred against one?—Good-bye—
We are great friends?

CYRANO. Yes, yes.

ROXANE. Tell him to write—
A hundred! You will tell me later. Now
I cannot stay. A hundred—oh, what courage.

CYRANO. [*Bows, and says bitterly to himself*] I have done better since.

[*She goes. He stands motionless.*]

RAGUENEAU. [*Enters, timidly*] Monsieur ——

CYRANO. Yes ——

RAGUENEAU. I ——

CYRANO. A glass of wine.

RAGUENEAU. Yes, Monsieur —— [*From a distance is heard faintly an old French marching song.* RAGUENEAU *returns with the wine, listens, then goes to window and looks out.*] Your friends, Monsieur, the Gascony cadets.

[*The music comes nearer, a company of eight pass the window and burst into the room, singing. They surround* CYRANO *eagerly.*]

CAPTAIN. Our hero.
CYRANO. [*Rises and salutes*] Our Captain.
RAGUENEAU. Are you all Gascons?
CADETS. All.
FIRST CADET. [*Embracing* CYRANO] Bravo.
CYRANO. Baron ——
SECOND CADET. Vivat ——
CYRANO. Baron ——
THIRD CADET. Let me hug you to my heart.
CYRANO. Baron ——
SEVERAL MORE. Let us hug him ——
CYRANO. Baron—Baron—pardon ——
RAGUENEAU. Messieurs,—are you all barons?
CADETS. All!
RAGUENEAU. [*To* CYRANO] Are they?
FIRST CADET. Our crests would build a tower to touch the clouds.

[LE BRET *rushes in.*]

LE BRET. [*To* CYRANO] My friend, the crowd is looking madly for you.
CYRANO. You did not tell them where I am?
LE BRET. [*Rubbing his hands*] I did.

[*The* MARQUIS *of* ACT I *comes running to* CYRANO *with outstretched hands, followed by a poet and a man of letters. More pass by the window.*]

RAGUENEAU. Monsieur, they come.—'Tis glorious.
CYRANO. Be quiet.
MARQUIS. [*To* CYRANO] My dear fellow ——
CYRANO. [*Drawing himself up haughtily*] Fellow? You're mistaken.
MARQUIS. [*Simpering*] But ——

CYRANO. You and I have naught in common, sir.
MARQUIS. Monsieur, I wish to present you to some ladies ——
CYRANO. [*Still haughtily*] By whom will you first be presented, pray? [*He looks coldly at the* MARQUIS *who retires amid some jeers by the crowd.*]
LE BRET. What is the matter with you, man ——?
CYRANO. Hush.

[RAGUENEAU *has been conversing with the poet and man of letters, and now presents each in turn to* CYRANO.]

MAN OF LETTERS. May I have the details?
CYRANO. No, Monsieur.
LE BRET. The inventor of the *Gazette*.
CYRANO. [*Sadly*] Ah, yes, the sheet
That tells so much—but—[*shrugs*] no matter.
LE BRET. Fool.
POET. [*To* CYRANO] Monsieur, I want to make a poem about you.
CYRANO. No!

[*All stare at him.* LE BRET *walks away impatiently.* DE GUICHE *enters, attended by* CUIGY *and* BRISSAILLE.]

CUIGY. [*To* CYRANO] Monsieur de Guiche.
DE GUICHE. [*Smiling and inclining his head*]
My admiration
For your latest feat.
LE BRET. [*Pleased*] Ah ——
CADETS. Bravo—bravo ——

[RAGUENEAU *places a chair for* DE GUICHE.]

DE GUICHE.
I would scarcely have believed the tale
Had not these gentlemen beheld the deed.

BRISSAILLE. With our own eyes.

[CYRANO *just stares.*]

DE GUICHE. A poet, too, who fights
And sings at once.

RAGUENEAU. [*Again imitating* CYRANO *in an imaginary duel*] I shall thrust when I end the refrain.

DE GUICHE.
You should be poet to some gentleman.
It is the vogue. Will you be mine?

CYRANO. No, sir.

DE GUICHE.
Your dash amused my uncle, Richelieu.
I could help you there.

LE BRET. Mon dieu! Perhaps
You'll get your "Agrippina" played, my friend.

DE GUICHE. Take it to him ——

CYRANO. You think ——

DE GUICHE. He is most expert;
He'll only change a line or two of yours.

CYRANO. [*Whose face immediately grows stern*]
Impossible, Monsieur, my blood runs cold
To think of changing even one small comma.

DE GUICHE. But when he likes a verse, my friend, he pays.

[*A* CADET *comes in with a collection of shabby hats spitted upon a sword.*]

CADET.
Look, Cyrano! This morning on the quay

What strangely feathered game we gathered in—
The hats left in the rout.

CAPTAIN. [*Laughing*] The spoils of war!

[*All laugh.*]

CUIGY.

Whoever hired this band of cutthroats
Is in a rage to-day.

BRISSAILLE. Is it known who?

DE GUICHE. [*Rises and speaks haughtily*]
'Twas I. [*Laughter ceases.*] I charged them to chastise—
A task
One does not do one's self—a drunken scribbler.

[*There is a constrained silence.*]

CAPTAIN. [*Taking hats from* CADET] What shall we make of them? A stew? They're greasy.

CYRANO. [*Takes sword on which they are impaled, salutes, and lets them all slip off at* DE GUICHE'S *feet*] Monsieur, will you return them to your friends?

DE GUICHE. [*Angrily*] My bearers and my chair—at once—I go! [*To* CYRANO.] You, sir ——

VOICES IN STREET. The bearers of my Lord Vicomte De Guiche ——

DE GUICHE. [*Continuing*] On you, sir, I will waste no words. [*He starts out haughtily, turns again.*] Monsieur, you have perhaps read Don Quixote?

CYRANO. Yes—
And find I like him well.—Sometimes I even
Fancy I am he.

DE GUICHE. The chapter on
The windmills?

CYRANO. Yes—chapter thirteen.

DE GUICHE. When one
Attacks them—it will oft befall ——

CYRANO. Then I
Attack folk turned by every wind?

DE GUICHE. [*Nods*] And while
Their sails in circles sweep about, Monsieur—
They'll land you in the mire ——

CYRANO. Or up among
The stars!

[*The* CADETS *laugh, but* CYRANO, *suddenly weary, sinks into a chair. The others hesitate, whisper, and go on talking ad lib. At a sign from* LE BRET *they go out in groups, wonderingly, disappointed at not hearing the story of the fight. When they are gone,* CYRANO *looks at* LE BRET.]

Well?

LE BRET. A nice thing you have done! Too bad!

CYRANO. Oh, come—stop grumbling, friend.

LE BRET. But, man, you ruin
Every chance that comes your way. It is too foolish!

CYRANO. I like extremes.

LE BRET. Then you exaggerate ——

CYRANO. Deliberately.

LE BRET. You are too reckless. Pray
Leave off a bit this guardsman's spirit.

CYRANO. Well,
What would you have me do, Le Bret? Would you
That I seek out some patron strong, and rise
By artifice and not by power?—No,
I thank you. Dedicate as others do

Verses to money lenders? Dress in motley
In hopes of seeing on a statesman's lips
A condescending smile? I thank you, no.
Shall I learn to grovel and to kneel
Or shall I show how limber is my back?
No, I thank you. On both shoulders carry water,
And sit the fence astraddle, while I flatter
Each to his face and feather my own nest?
No, I thank you. Be the little great man
Of a clique? Sail with madrigals
For oars and sighs of wealthy dames for winds?
Pay for publishing my poems?—No,
I thank you and again I thank you.—But
To dream—to laugh—to sing—to go about
Alone and free with eyes that face life squarely,
With voice that rings with joy of combat—yes—
To wear my hat just as I choose—to fight—
Or write—to win, without a hope of glory:
Fly to the moon in fancy if I wish—
Nor sing one line that comes not from my heart,
And yet be modest. To tell myself, "My soul,
Content yourself with flowers and fruits—with
  leaves—
If you have gathered them in your garden."
Then if by chance I gain some small success,
No tribute money need I pay to Cæsar—
All the honor is mine own. Good friend,
I am too proud to be a parasite,
And if I lack the power to tower like
An oak or a great mountain pine, I still
Must feel that though I do not rise so high,
At least I go unaided and alone.

LE BRET.

Alone—so be it! But why against the world?

How did you get this mad idea of yours
Of making enemies where'er you go?

CYRANO.
By watching you make friends. I will not bow
To condescending smiles, and when disdainful
Faces turn away, I cry, "Thank God,
Another enemy."

LE BRET. But this is madness!

CYRANO.
Well, yes, perhaps. And yet it is my pleasure.
To know that I am hated pleases me;
To face the fusillade of angry eyes
And know my doublet's spattered o'er by Envy
Stirs my blood. In short, Hate sheathes me; gives
To me a ruff that holds my head erect.
Every new enemy another pleat—
A new constraint at once a collar—and—
A halo.

LE BRET. [*After a pause, puts his arm through* CYRANO'S]
Tell this to all the world—but not to me—
To me, your friend, whisper softly that
She loves you not ——!

[*The* CADETS *again burst in.*]

CYRANO. [*Sharply*] Hush!

[CHRISTIAN *passes the window and enters alone.*]

FIRST CADET. Cyrano—the story!

CYRANO. In a moment —— [*He withdraws on* LE BRET'S *arm.*]

[*The* CADETS *gather around the table.* RAGUENEAU *waits on them.* CHRISTIAN *joins them.*]

SECOND CADET.

The story of the fight! 'Twill be a lesson
For this untried recruit.

CHRISTIAN. Untried recruit?

SECOND CADET. Yes, northern weakling ——

CHRISTIAN. Weakling, did you say?

SECOND CADET.

Monsieur de Neuvillette—learn this at once.
There is one thing we do not mention. [*He looks around mysteriously and points to his nose three times.*]

CHRISTIAN. Ah,
'Tis his ——

SECOND CADET. Hush! That word is never uttered.
[*Points to* CYRANO *who is talking to* LE BRET *in the background.*]
Or 'tis with him there you will have to do.

THIRD CADET.

He slew two men because he liked it not
That they talked through their noses.

FOURTH CADET. Just a word
Alluding to that fatal feature's—death ——

FIRST CADET.

Word?—a gesture is enough.—Why, man—
To draw one's kerchief is to draw one's shroud.

CHRISTIAN. [*Rises and walks toward the* CAPTAIN *while the* CADETS *fold their arms and watch in silence*]
Captain!

CAPTAIN. Monsieur?

CHRISTIAN. What is the thing to do
When Southrons grow too boastful?

CAPTAIN. Prove to them
One can be from the North, and still be brave.

CHRISTIAN. I thank you.

FIRST CADET. Cyrano—your story now ——

ALL. Yes, yes,—the story.

CYRANO. [*Coming forward*]
What, my story?—Well ——

[*All draw near.* CHRISTIAN *straddles a chair and looks up expectantly.*]

I was marching all alone to meet them;
The moon shone in the sky like a great watch
Of silver, when suddenly it was as if
A careful watchmaker first drew a piece
Of cloudy cotton across the shining crystal.
Night came—the darkest night in all the world;
You could not see ——

CHRISTIAN. [*Impudently*] Beyond your nose.

CADETS. Oh!

CYRANO. Who is that man?

FIRST CADET. He is the man who came
This morning.

CYRANO. [*Taking a step toward* CHRISTIAN] Did you say this morning?

CAPTAIN. Baron de Neuvil ——

CYRANO. [*Falling back*]
Ah—'tis well—

[*Makes another move toward* CHRISTIAN, *regains his composure, and continues in a quiet voice.*]

Well—
As I was saying —— [*With a burst of anger.*]
Mon dieu!—

[*Then again in a natural tone.*]

You could not see—

[CADETS *show great amazement.*]

And so I went, thinking that for a beggar

I was about to offend some mighty prince—
Who would surely make me pay ——

CHRISTIAN. With your nose?

CYRANO. [*Goes up to him, stares, and makes a gesture of contempt*]
But I said—Forward, do your duty,
Gascon—march. Then onward in the dark
I go, and feel ——

CHRISTIAN. A filip on the nose.

CYRANO. I parry. Suddenly I find myself ——

CHRISTIAN. Nose against nose ——

CYRANO. [*Leaping at him*] Ventre Saint Gris!
[*All rush forward to see, but when he reaches* CHRISTIAN, *he regains his self-control and continues.*]
With a hundred
Roistering ruffians. So—I charge. Before
I knew it—I was ——

CHRISTIAN. Nose to nose ——

CYRANO. On them.
Two I rip up! I run another through!
Then someone lunges—Paf! I answer ——

CHRISTIAN. Pif!

CYRANO. Death and damnation! Out with you all—out!

FIRST CADET. [*As all rush to door, talking quickly as they go*] The tiger wakes ——

CYRANO. Leave me with this man.

SECOND CADET. We'll find him cut in mincemeat ——

RAGUENEAU. What! In mincemeat?

THIRD CADET. Filling for your patties ——

CAPTAIN. Let us go.

FOURTH CADET. He will not leave a single morsel of him.

FIRST CADET. I die of fright to think what will befall!

SECOND CADET. Terrible!

[*When the door has closed,* CYRANO *and* CHRISTIAN *stand looking at each other for a moment.*]

CYRANO. [*Holding out his arms*] Come to my arms!

CHRISTIAN. Monsieur?

CYRANO. Come.

CHRISTIAN. But ——

CYRANO. You have courage. That pleases me.

CHRISTIAN. But tell ——

CYRANO. Your hand. I am her brother.

CHRISTIAN. Whose?

CYRANO. Hers!

CHRISTIAN. What?

CYRANO. Roxane's.

CHRISTIAN. Heavens! You—her brother ——?

CYRANO. Yes — or almost. Her cousin — like a brother ——

CHRISTIAN. She told you ——?

CYRANO. All ——

CHRISTIAN. She loves me?

CYRANO. Yes.

CHRISTIAN. Ah!—[*He stands for a moment in blissful silence, then puts out his hand to* CYRANO.] Monsieur, I am so happy to have met you.

CYRANO. This is what might be called a sudden friendship.

CHRISTIAN. Forgive me.

CYRANO. [*Looking at him and putting a hand on his shoulder*] True, he is a handsome rascal.

CHRISTIAN. If you knew, Monsieur, how I admire you!

CYRANO. But all those " noses " which ——

CHRISTIAN. I take them back ——

CYRANO. Roxane to-night expects a letter ——

CHRISTIAN. Ah!

CYRANO. What?

CHRISTIAN.
I shall spoil my chances if I speak.
I am so stupid—that I die for shame.

CYRANO.
No, you are not, since you take count of it.
And your attack on me was not so stupid.

CHRISTIAN.
Bah—it takes no wit to pick a quarrel—
And I may have a ready soldier's wit,
But with a woman I am speechless.

CYRANO. Yes?

CHRISTIAN. 'Tis true their eyes look kindly on me ——

CYRANO. And
Their hearts?

CHRISTIAN. No, no—I never can make love.
Oh, for the power to express what I feel here.
[*Puts hand on heart.*]

CYRANO. Oh, to be a handsome musketeer.

CHRISTIAN. Roxane has wit! I'll kill all her illusions!

CYRANO. [*Looking at* CHRISTIAN] Ah—if my soul were clothed in such a body.

CHRISTIAN. If I had but your gift of words.

CYRANO. Then, come,
I'll lend you mine. Together we will make
One hero of romance.

CHRISTIAN. What?

CYRANO. You'll speak
Each day the words I'll teach you.

CHRISTIAN. You suggest ——

CYRANO.
Roxane shall never lose her fond illusions.

We two shall win her heart as one—for I
From my buff jerkin to your broidered doublet
Shall breathe my very soul.

CHRISTIAN. But, Cyrano ——

CYRANO. You will?

CHRISTIAN. You frighten me.

CYRANO. A simple plan—
You'll go ahead—and I, your shadow, always
At your side. You'll be the fairy prince—
And I—the kiss, with which you win her heart.

CHRISTIAN. Your eyes are gleaming!

CYRANO. Will you?

CHRISTIAN. Yes—but you ——?

CYRANO. It will amuse me.

CHRISTIAN. But the letter ——

CYRANO. [*Hands him a letter*] Here.

CHRISTIAN. I ——

CYRANO. Send it.—Do not fear. We poets
Have dream mistresses to whom we write
Confessions and avowals. Take it. Change
These fancies into facts.

CHRISTIAN. But, Roxane?—Will
It fit Roxane?

CYRANO. 'Twill fit her like a glove.
Roxane will think 'twas written all for her.

CHRISTIAN. My friend! [*He throws himself into* CYRANO'S *arms and they stand embracing each other. The door partly opens.*]

FIRST CADET. No word.—The silence of the grave.

[*The rest come in.*]

OTHERS. What is this?—Behold!—Why—Cyrano!

CAPTAIN.
Mild as a saint our devil has become!
Smitten upon one cheek, he turns the other.

SECOND CADET. [*Smelling the air*]
This odor—[*Approaches* CYRANO.]
Sir, have you not noticed it?
What does it smell of here? Something dead?

CYRANO. [*Boxing his ears*] Blockheads!

(CYRANO *Theme.*)

[CADETS *rejoice that* CYRANO *has not changed. One turns somersaults, others embrace each other in joy, others attempt to embrace* CYRANO, *who holds them off in mock anger.*]

CURTAIN

ACT III

(*LIGHTS—Bright twilight. Amber street lamp up* L.)

(*Godard's "Chanson Florian." Tenor with guitar. First stanza before rise of curtain.*)

SCENE: *A small square in the old Marais. To the* R., ROXANE'S *house with balcony and a door. A bench* L. C. *The house on* L. *may be suggested by hedge or stairs. The* DUENNA *is seated on the bench. A minstrel passes by, singing, comes up to* DUENNA *who gives him money. He goes on, and a lady passes and goes up-stairs* L., *bowing to* DUENNA.

(*Music fades.*)

DUENNA. Roxane, are you ready? We are late.
ROXANE. [*From within*] I am coming.
CYRANO. [*Off stage*] La-la-la-la ——
DUENNA. Roxane.
ROXANE. Coming.
CYRANO. [*Enters*] Ah, Madame ——
ROXANE. [*From window*] Ah, Cyrano —— [*He looks up and bows.*] I'll be down. [*She goes into house.*]
CYRANO. [*To* DUENNA] Then you are going out?
DUENNA.
Clomire receives to-night. We are to hear
A discourse on the tender passion.
CYRANO. Ah ——

[*More ladies pass and go up-stairs* L.]

ROXANE. [*Enters and holds out her hand.* CYRANO *bends to kiss it*] 'Tis you.

CYRANO. 'Tis I—come to salute your lilies,
And pay my compliments to—[*pause*] your roses.

ROXANE. Nothing else?

CYRANO. Ah, yes—as every night,
To ask if he—your friend—is still perfection.

ROXANE. Still—the friend of my soul. How I love him!

CYRANO. [*Smiling*] Christian has wit?

ROXANE. Yes, better, cousin, e'en
Than yours!

CYRANO. Of course.

ROXANE. I think there could not be
A better framer of those pretty nothings
That are everything. Sometimes, 'tis true,
His muse deserts him—he's distraught—I tremble—
Then—suddenly he speaks—enchantingly—
Once more.

CYRANO. Really? [*A tinge of satire.*]

ROXANE. Oh, fie! How like a man!
Because Baron de Neuvillette is good
To look upon, you say he has no wit.

CYRANO. Does he talk well of matters of the heart?

ROXANE.
Listen! "Take my heart. The more you take,
The more I have. But since, to suffer, I
Must have a heart—I pray you—send me yours."

CYRANO.
Sometimes he has too little—then too much—
How much does he desire?

ROXANE. You anger me,
Monsieur. I see that you are jealous!

CYRANO. Jealous?

ROXANE.
Of a fellow poet, who quite eats
You up. But this—the tenderest of them all—
"Believe me that my heart makes but one cry—
To you; so through the words I write I send
You kisses, dear. Pray read my letter with
Your lips."

CYRANO. [*Smiling in spite of himself*] Ha-ha! Those lines are—[*stopping himself, he finishes disdainfully*] pretty weak.

ROXANE. And this ——

CYRANO. [*Delighted*] You know his letters, then, by heart?

ROXANE. Every one.

CYRANO. Truly, that is flattering ——

ROXANE. He is a master ——

CYRANO. Oh—a master!

ROXANE. [*Peremptorily*] Yes.

CYRANO. Well, so be it, then—he is a master.

DUENNA. [*Advancing to* CYRANO]
Monsieur de Guiche. Go in—perhaps, 'twere better—
He should not see you here ——

ROXANE. Yes—yes—my love
Is yet a tender blossom. He loves me, too.
He must not guess—for he has power to deal
My love a cruel stroke.

CYRANO. Oh, very well. [*He goes into the house.*]

ROXANE. [*Curtseying to* DE GUICHE] Monsieur de Guiche.

(*Twilight gradually deepens.*)

DE GUICHE. I came to take my leave.

ROXANE. You go away?

DE GUICHE. To war!

ROXANE. Ah!

DE GUICHE. Yes—to-night.

ROXANE. Ah!

DE GUICHE. I am under orders. We besiege
Arras.

ROXANE. A siege?

DE GUICHE. [*Nods*] I see that my departure
Leaves you cold.

ROXANE. Oh, no ——

DE GUICHE. Well, as for me—
I'm in despair! When shall we meet again?
You know they've made me colonel ——

ROXANE. [*Indifferently*] Bravo.

DE GUICHE. Of the Guards.

ROXANE. [*Suddenly interested*] The Guards?

DE GUICHE. The regiment
In which your cousin serves—that braggart bold—
I shall have my revenge on him down there.

ROXANE. [*Choking*] The Guards are going?

DE GUICHE. [*Smiling*] 'Tis my regiment.

ROXANE. [*Falling back on the bench*] Christian!

DE GUICHE. What is the matter?

ROXANE. This—departure—
Will break my heart. To care for anyone—
And know him at the war ——

DE GUICHE. [*Surprised and charmed*]
Then you do care?
You tell me kindly—now, for the first time—
The day I go away —— It is too cruel ——

ROXANE. [*Changing her tone*]
Tell me, you say you wish to be revenged
On Cyrano, my cousin?

DE GUICHE. You plead for him?

ROXANE. No—I would urge you on—against him.

DE GUICHE. [*Surprised*] Yes?
You see him ——?

ROXANE. [*Shrugs*] Seldom.

DE GUICHE. One meets him everywhere
With one young Neuvillette ——

ROXANE. A tall man ——

DE GUICHE. Blond—
Handsome ——

ROXANE. Pooh!

DE GUICHE. But somewhat stupid ——

ROXANE. [*Controls herself*] Yes.
But your revenge on Cyrano? You think
To order him to war? That, Monsieur,
Would please him—he delights in danger—'tis
His life. I know the way to break his heart.

DE GUICHE. You know ——?

ROXANE. [*Nods*] Leave him behind—and his
Cadets—to fold their arms in Paris—here—
While all the rest march off to war.
He'll eat his heart out! And his friends will gnaw
Their fists, and you will be avenged, Monsieur.

DE GUICHE.
Only a woman could think of this!—You love
Me then, a little? [ROXANE *smiles.*] In taking up my grudge—
I fain would see a proof of love—Roxane ——

ROXANE. Perhaps it is.

DE GUICHE. [*Takes out sealed packets*]
The orders will be sent
This moment to each troop—except—this one—
For the Cadets—I keep. [*He smiles.*] Ah, Cyrano—
This time the game is mine.

ROXANE. And mine. [*They laugh.*]

DE GUICHE. I love
You to distraction. Listen. This evening ——

ROXANE. But ——

DE GUICHE. I know I ought to go.

ROXANE. Yes—yes —— You must ——

DE GUICHE.
When, for the first time, you admit you care?
I have a plan—the good Capuchin fathers
Are servants of my Uncle Cardinal.
They will be my friends and shelter me.
People will think me gone—I'll come in mask ——

ROXANE. But if you are discovered!—Your honor!

DE GUICHE. Bah!

ROXANE. Your duty as a soldier ——

DE GUICHE. Cannot be helped.
Pray let me ——

ROXANE. No ——

DE GUICHE. Yes ——

ROXANE. [*With feigned hesitation*]
I should forbid you—
Love itself bids me forbid you ——

DE GUICHE. Love?

ROXANE. [*Nods*]
Go—I pray—for my sake—be a hero,
Antoine —— [*She whispers his name softly.*]

DE GUICHE. My name upon your lips?—Roxane!
You love ——

ROXANE. The one for whose dear sake I tremble ——

DE GUICHE. Ah! I will go! [*Kissing her hand.*]
But say you are content?

ROXANE. I am, my friend, I am.

[*He goes.*]

DUENNA. [*Making a mock curtsey*]
We are, Monsieur—
We are —— Roxane—come. We shall miss the discourse
Of—oh, the tender passion! [*She looks off as sounds of laughter and talking come from house* L. *They start toward it.*]

ROXANE. Not a word
To Cyrano. I've stolen his war, and he
Will not forgive me.
[CYRANO *comes out of* ROXANE'S *house, sees her, and comes over as she is going up the stairs.*]
If Christian comes,
Tell him to wait.

CYRANO. When he comes, what will
You talk about? You always know beforehand.

ROXANE. About ——

CYRANO. Well?

ROXANE. You will not tell him?

CYRANO. I
Am dumb.

ROXANE. About nothing—or everything.
I shall say, "Speak of love in your own words ——"

CYRANO. Good ——

ROXANE. Sh!
CYRANO. Sh!
ROXANE. Not a word.
CYRANO. Thank you so much!
ROXANE. He must be unprepared.
CYRANO. Of course ——
ROXANE. Sh!
CYRANO. Sh!

[*She goes in.* CYRANO *looks after her.* CHRISTIAN *enters.*]

CHRISTIAN. You ——
CYRANO. Christian!
CHRISTIAN. Yes—I wait upon Roxane.
CYRANO. But first—come to where I lodge. I'll teach you ——
CHRISTIAN. No!
CYRANO. What?
CHRISTIAN. I tell you, "No." I'm sick of borrowing.
Sick of playing this timid part. I know
'Twas good at first. But now I feel she loves me,
I'm not afraid.. Henceforth, I'll speak myself.
CYRANO. Ah!
CHRISTIAN. I'm not so stupid after all—you'll see!
Besides, my friend, I've learned a lot from you.
I can speak quite alone! And by the gods—
One thing I can do—take her in my arms.
[*A laugh is heard.*]
'Tis she!—No—do not leave me—Cyrano.
CYRANO. [*Bowing*] Speak quite alone, Monsieur.

[GUESTS *begin to come down from* L. ROXANE *and* DUENNA *come on.*]

ROXANE. We were too late.

DUENNA. We've missed the discourse on the tender passion.

CYRANO. Adieu —— [*He nods in the direction of* CHRISTIAN, *who, for one terrible moment, has stepped behind a tree, and now comes forth.*]

ROXANE. Mon dieu! 'Tis you! [*She takes both his hands.*]

[CYRANO *whispers to* DUENNA *and departs.* CHRISTIAN *is so enraptured that he doesn't see the* DUENNA, *who sails past them indignantly, then turns at the door.*]

(*Gradually bring up Blue Spot on Bench.*)

DUENNA. Bon soir, Monsieur.

[*He turns, starts, sees her and is confused.* ROXANE *laughs, takes his hand and leads him to the bench.*]

ROXANE.

They are gone! Come—no one is near ——
Sit down.
Speak—I am listening ——

CHRISTIAN. I love you ——

ROXANE. [*Closing her eyes*] Yes—
Talk of love —— [*Sighs.*]

CHRISTIAN. I love you dearly—I ——

ROXANE. That is the theme. Now improvise.

CHRISTIAN. I love you ——

ROXANE. What — again? — The same? — Variations, please.

CHRISTIAN. I love you so ——

ROXANE. I do not doubt it—but ——

CHRISTIAN. Tell me, Roxane, do you love me? Tell me.

ROXANE. [*Disgustedly*] Explain a little how you love.

CHRISTIAN. So much!

ROXANE. Of course—and then ——
CHRISTIAN. And then—I'd be so glad—
If you loved me!
ROXANE. A song! A melody—
Cease playing on a single string.
CHRISTIAN. Your neck—
Roxane—I should so love to kiss it ——
ROXANE. Christian!
CHRISTIAN. I love you ——
ROXANE. [*Starting up*] Once again ——
CHRISTIAN. [*Quickly holding her back*] I love you not ——
ROXANE. [*Sitting down*] Ah—that is better.
CHRISTIAN. I adore you ——
ROXANE. Oh ——
CHRISTIAN. I grow a fool ——
ROXANE. And that displeases me.
It is as though you suddenly grew ugly.
CHRISTIAN. Roxane, believe ——
ROXANE. Be eloquent ——
CHRISTIAN. I love ——
ROXANE.
I know you love me. That is not enough.
Adieu ——
CHRISTIAN. Wait, please—and hear ——
ROXANE. That you adore me?
I know that, too.
CHRISTIAN. I—I ——
ROXANE. Go away. [*She goes in and closes door.*]
CHRISTIAN. Roxane ——
CYRANO. [*Enters*] A great success!
CHRISTIAN. Help me.
CYRANO. Not I.
CHRISTIAN. I pray.

CYRANO. No, sir.
CHRISTIAN. But I shall die unless at once
I win her smiles again ——

(*Candle in Balcony Window. Gradually dim Bench Spot and bring up Blue Spot on Balcony.*)

CYRANO. And how the devil
Can I teach you to do it on the spot?
[*Then, seeing a light in her window.*]
Her window!
CHRISTIAN. I shall die ——
CYRANO. Hush!
CHRISTIAN. I shall die!
CYRANO. The night is dark ——
CHRISTIAN. Well?
CYRANO. You do not deserve
My help.
CHRISTIAN. I pray ——
CYRANO. Hush. Stand there—be quick.
Beneath her balcony, I'll prompt.
CHRISTIAN. But ——
CYRANO. Hush—
Fool—hold your tongue.
[*He throws a pebble.* ROXANE *peers out, then opens the window.*]
Call her.
CHRISTIAN. Roxane!
ROXANE. Who calls?
CHRISTIAN. I ——
ROXANE. Who ——?
CHRISTIAN. Christian.
ROXANE. [*With disdain*] Is it you?
CHRISTIAN. I would speak ——
ROXANE. Again? Oh, no, you speak too ill. Be gone!

CHRISTIAN. Roxane ——

ROXANE. You do not love me any more.

CHRISTIAN.

Ye gods—you say I love no more, when I
Love most.

[ROXANE, *about to close window, hesitates, and he continues, prompted by* CYRANO.]

Love, cradled in my restless soul,
Becomes a Hercules with strength enough
In infancy to strangle those two serpents,
Doubt and Pride. [*He stammers through this.*]

ROXANE. Better—but tell me, pray,
Why do you speak your words so falteringly?

CYRANO. [*Pulls* CHRISTIAN *under balcony and glides into his place, taking care to stand in shadow*]

Hush!

[*Continuing to* ROXANE, *imitating* CHRISTIAN'S *voice.*]

Because it now is night; and in
The dark, they grope about to find your ear.

ROXANE. But mine encounter no such obstacles.

CYRANO.

Ah, no. For I receive them in my heart:
My heart is large—your ear is wondrous small.
Besides, your words descend—their pace is swift,
While mine must climb.

ROXANE. But now in these last moments
It seems ——

CYRANO. [*Interrupting*] They've learned the way.

ROXANE. I'm coming down.

CYRANO. No ——

ROXANE. But ——

CYRANO. Do not come down.

ROXANE. But not to see ——

CYRANO.

Is sheer delight. You see the trailing blackness
Of a cloak, and I, the whiteness of
A woman's summer robe. I am a shadow,
You, a radiance.

ROXANE. You have another voice ——

CYRANO.

Yes—for in the sheltering night, I dare
To be myself.

ROXANE. Yourself?

CYRANO. Why, yes. Sincere
Without constraint or fear ——

ROXANE. Fear? Of what?

CYRANO. Of being mocked about—my ardor ——

ROXANE. Ah!

CYRANO.

I start to snatch a star—but stop in fear
Of ridicule—to pluck a little flower.

ROXANE. Monsieur, the flower has charms ——

CYRANO. But not enough
For you and me to-night.

ROXANE. You never spoke
To me like this ——

CYRANO. [*Passionately*] You've never heard till now
My own heart speaking.—Roxane—your name to me
Is like a bell hung in my trembling heart—
A bell that swings and rings, "Roxane," "Roxane,"—
And everything you do lives in my heart;
Last year, one day, in going out at morn
You changed the fashion of your hair—your hair
That has the golden brightness of the sun,

But as I gazed, my eyes were blinded by
The radiant light of you—my sun.

ROXANE. My love—
For this is love ——

CYRANO. Yes, verily. The love
That does not seek its own, but gives itself
Ungrudgingly, and only asks to hear
The distant laughter of your happiness,
And feel, perhaps, it was Love's gift to you.
Believe me, when I say with every look
From your dear eyes new courage springs to life
In me—new valor. Ah—you understand
A little, and feel my soul climb slowly through
The dark? Ah—this night is all too fair
And sweet—I tell you of my love—and you—
You listen. It is too much. Roxane, I feel
You tremble.—What is death like, I wonder?— Now
All else I know.—You tremble—at my words—
My voice—I feel your trembling hand come down
To me — come down, along these jasmine branches ——
[*He madly catches the end of a vine hanging from the balcony and kisses it.*]
Ah ——!

ROXANE. I tremble—I weep—I love thee—I am thine.

CYRANO.
I have lived—now let death come at once.
I ask but one thing more ——

CHRISTIAN. A kiss!

ROXANE. One ——?

CYRANO. [*To* CHRISTIAN] You ——!

ROXANE. You ask me ——

CYRANO. Yes, but—I mean —— [*To* CHRISTIAN.]
You go too far—
Hush!

CHRISTIAN. Since she's moved, I must improve my chance ——

CYRANO. [*To* ROXANE] I did ask, but I know I ask too much.

ROXANE. One kiss—too much?

CYRANO. I beg you grant it not.

CHRISTIAN. Why—why ——

CYRANO. Hush, Christian ——!

ROXANE. What is that you say?

CYRANO.
I scold myself for having gone too far,
And to myself I say, "Hush, Christian,"—wait ——
[*A* CAPUCHIN *with lantern enters, looking about in the darkness.*]
Who's this new follower of Diogenes?

[ROXANE *goes in.*]

CAPUCHIN. The house of Madame ——

CHRISTIAN. Send him away.

CAPUCHIN. Robin?

CYRANO. Go straight ahead—that way —— [*Pointing off* L.]

CAPUCHIN. Thank you, I'll say
For you a prayer, Monsieur. [*He goes off.*]

CHRISTIAN. The kiss ——

CYRANO. No.

CHRISTIAN. But ——

ROXANE. [*Opening window*] Are you there? You were speaking of ——

CYRANO. A kiss.

ROXANE. A kiss?

CYRANO. What is a kiss? It is a promise—
Or a vow—a rosy dot upon
The *i* of *loving*—a secret breathed from lip
To lip like the sweet breath of flowers, in that
Immortal moment when soul communes with soul.

ROXANE. Be still!

CYRANO. But why? The Queen of France, Madame,
The Queen herself let her most happy courtier
Take one ——

ROXANE. Well!

CYRANO. I worship you, my Queen—
Like him, I'm sad and faithful ——

ROXANE. And like him
You're fair ——

CYRANO. [*Aside*] I'm fair:—I quite forgot ——

ROXANE. Climb—and be made glad ——

CYRANO. [*Pushing* CHRISTIAN *to the vines hanging from the balcony*] Climb ——

ROXANE. This promise ——

CYRANO. Climb ——

CHRISTIAN. Perhaps I'd better not ——

CYRANO. Climb, fool ——

CHRISTIAN. [*Climbs to balustrade, which he vaults*] Roxane! [*Kisses her.*]

CYRANO. I've won what I have won.—Yet now,
At the feast of love, I am but Lazarus—
And still I feel my heart has something gained,
For 'tis my words upon his lips she kisses.

[*From the distance the minstrel's song is heard.* CYRANO *tiptoes away from beneath the balcony, then pretends to be just entering.*]

Ho—there!

(" *Chanson Florian.*")

(*Gradually bring up Bench Spot again.*)

ROXANE. What is it?

CYRANO. It is I—just passing—
Christian still there?

CHRISTIAN. What—Cyrano?

ROXANE. Good-evening,
Cousin!

(*Music fades.*)

CYRANO. Cousin, good-evening!

ROXANE. I'm coming down.

[*The* CAPUCHIN *reënters.*]

CHRISTIAN. Again!

CAPUCHIN. 'Tis here—I'm sure—Madeleine Robin ——

CYRANO. You said Rolin ——

CAPUCHIN. No—" bin "—" bin "——

ROXANE. What is it?

CAPUCHIN. A letter ——

CHRISTIAN. What?

CAPUCHIN. Oh, it might be
About some holy matter. It was a lord—
A worthy lord who ——

ROXANE. It is de Guiche!

CHRISTIAN. He dares!

ROXANE.
Oh—but he will not trouble me forever.
[*She unseals letter and reads.*]
" Mademoiselle—the drums beat loud—my soldiers
Go to war. I stay—I must see you—
You smiled too kindly on me. Pray, bid all
Be gone and graciously receive a man
Too bold—yet pardoned, may I hope?—who signs

Himself ——" Father, listen to the letter—
[CAPUCHIN *turns from* CYRANO, *who has been talking to him.*]
"Mademoiselle, we must submit ourselves
To the Cardinal's will—hard though it be for you.
I send this man, a holy monk, to you
With the blessing of the church. Forthwith—e'en though
You like him not—you must marry Christian;
Then be resigned, and Heaven's blessing be yours.
Your very humble ——"

CAPUCHIN. The worthy lord! I thought
It was some holy errand.

ROXANE. [*To* CHRISTIAN] Do I read well?
[*Then aloud.*]
'Tis frightful.

CAPUCHIN. [*Turning his lantern on* CYRANO] Is it you?

CHRISTIAN. 'Tis I.

CAPUCHIN. [*In surprise*] But why ——

ROXANE. [*Interrupting*] Post Scriptum:—Give six score gold pistoles to the convent.

CAPUCHIN. [*Delighted*] Worthy—worthy lord. [*Then to* ROXANE.] Resign yourself, my child.

ROXANE. [*Assuming the air of a martyr*]
I am resigned. [*Then to* CYRANO.]
Cousin, you must help. Detain de Guiche—
He is coming:—let him not come in before ——

CYRANO. I understand. [*To the monk.*] To bless them takes how long?

CAPUCHIN. Ten minutes ——

CHRISTIAN. My friend ——

CYRANO. [*Frowning*] Go—I stay.

CHRISTIAN. But ——

CYRANO. Go.

[*All enter house.*]

Now—for de Guiche—and how to keep him out.

[*Walks up and down, thinking.*]

There—my plan is made.—Holloa—a man.

DE GUICHE. [*Enters, masked, feeling his way in the night*]

'Tis there—I cannot see—this mask annoys me.

[CYRANO *has prostrated himself on the ground.* DE GUICHE *tries to get past, but* CYRANO *prevents him from doing so.*]

Well—what is this? You've fallen ——

CYRANO. From the moon ——

DE GUICHE. From the ——?

CYRANO. [*In a dreamy voice*] What time is it?

DE GUICHE. He's lost his mind.

CYRANO. What country—what o'clock—what day—what season?

DE GUICHE. But ——

CYRANO. I am dazed.

DE GUICHE. Monsieur ——

CYRANO. For like a bomb

I've fallen from the moon!

DE GUICHE. [*Impatiently*] Yes, but Monsieur ——

CYRANO. [*Getting up, with a terrible voice*] Thence have I fallen ——

DE GUICHE. [*Drawing back*]

Yes, yes, thence you've fallen ——

[*Aside.*]

Perhaps he is a madman.

CYRANO. [*Advancing toward him*] And my fall

It is no metaphor!

DE GUICHE. But ——

CYRANO. A century since,
Or else a moment—I was—there—[*points*] in the moon.

DE GUICHE. Yes—let me pass ——

CYRANO. [*Standing in his way*] Where am I?—Tell me frankly.

DE GUICHE. The devil!

CYRANO. I could not choose my landing place.
Am I in a moon—or in a world ——?

DE GUICHE. But, sir—I ——

CYRANO. Ha—ye gods! Your face is black.
Can this be Africa? Are you a native?

DE GUICHE. [*Feeling his mask*] This mask ——

CYRANO. [*Somewhat reassured*] Or is this Genoa or Venice?

DE GUICHE. [*Trying to pass*] A lady waits for me ——

CYRANO. [*With a happy smile*] So this is Paris.

DE GUICHE. [*Smiling in spite of himself*] He's an amusing fellow ——

CYRANO. Ah—you laugh?

DE GUICHE. I laugh—but wish to pass.

CYRANO. [*Beaming*] How good to be
In Paris.

[*Entirely at his ease, he brushes himself and bows.*]

I came—pardon—in the whirlwind—
The ether clings to me—I've traveled far—
My eyes are filled with star dust. On my spurs
I still have shreds torn from a planet's hide—

[*Picking at his sleeve.*]

See—on my doublet—there's a comet's hair!

[*Puffs as if to blow it away.*]

DE GUICHE. Monsieur —— [*As he tries to pass,*

CYRANO *holds out his leg as if to show him something.*]

CYRANO. See—in my boot—I bring a tooth
From the Great Bear.
[DE GUICHE *again tries to pass.* CYRANO *holds his coat.*]
If you should strike my nose,
It would drip milk!

DE GUICHE. [*Interested in spite of himself*] Milk?

CYRANO. From the Milky Way.

DE GUICHE. Hell!

CYRANO. Oh, no, Monsieur—I come from heaven.
[*Folds his arms.*]
Curious—would you believe—[*laughs*] I saw—up there—
That Sirius wears a nightcap. Yes—indeed;
And the Little Bear is still too young to bite;
And as I crossed the Lyre, I broke a string ——

DE GUICHE. But ——

CYRANO. Ah, yes, you wish to hear of what
The moon is made, and if folk dwell on it?

DE GUICHE. No—no—I wish ——

CYRANO. To know how I ascended?

DE GUICHE. I say ——

CYRANO. I did not use the stupid eagle
Of Regiomontanus, nor the dove
Archytas used ——

DE GUICHE. [*Surprised*] He's mad!—but very learned ——

CYRANO.
I followed naught that has been done before ——
[DE GUICHE *has passed, but* CYRANO *follows, ready to lay hold of him.*]

Three ways did I invent to violate
The virgin sky.

DE GUICHE. [*Again interested in spite of himself*] Really?

CYRANO. [*Quickly*] I deck
My naked body with vials filled up to the brim
With tears dropped from the morning sky; and so
I am drawn upward by the sun that drinks
Each day the dew.

DE GUICHE. [*Surprised and interested*] Yes—that makes one.

CYRANO. [*Drawing back to get him to the other side*] And then—
Since smoke must surely rise aloft, I blow
Into a globe enough to bear me up.
[DE GUICHE *follows with interest.*]
Or, seated on an iron plate, I throw
A magnet in the air. The iron follows,
And again I throw the magnet—again
I rise, and so continue without end.
[*He has been leading* DE GUICHE *to the other side of the bench.*]

DE GUICHE. [*With satisfaction*] That's three—all good—and which did you adopt?

CYRANO. I chose a fourth ——

DE GUICHE. And that?

CYRANO. You'd never guess ——

DE GUICHE. The rascal grows interesting now.

[CYRANO *makes a noise like waves, with a great, mysterious gesture.*]

CYRANO. Hoouh!—Hoouh!

DE GUICHE. Well?

CYRANO. You guess?

DE GUICHE. No.

CYRANO. The tide!
At the hour when the moon does draw the wave,
I bathed me in the spray and lay upon
The sand—I rose in air—head up, because
The hair retains the moisture—softly, gently,
I ascended—then—[DE GUICHE, *carried away by curiosity, sits down on the bench*] then—[*in his own voice*] the time is up.
I'll let you go—the marriage is made.

(*Gradually bring up Reds in Footlights and Borders.*)

DE GUICHE. What! Am I then drunk—whose voice is this? [ROXANE'S *door opens and* LACKEYS *appear with lighted candelabra.* CYRANO *takes off his hat.*] This nose!—Cyrano ——

CYRANO. [*Bows*] Cyrano.
This very moment they've exchanged the rings.

DE GUICHE. They ——? [*He turns. Behind the* LACKEYS, ROXANE *and* CHRISTIAN *hold hands. The* CAPUCHIN *follows them, smiling. The* DUENNA *closes the line.*] He wins. [*To* ROXANE.] You? [*Recognizing* CHRISTIAN.] He!—A clever stroke. [*To* CYRANO.]
My compliments. Your story would have made
A saint stop short at Heaven's gate. Monsieur,
Remember the details; they'll make a book.

[CYRANO *bows.*]

CAPUCHIN. A handsome pair, my son, that you have joined.

DE GUICHE. [*Coldly*]
Yes—and now, Madame, I beg that you
Will bid farewell to your husband.

ROXANE. Farewell?

DE GUICHE. Of course—he goes to war. [*To* CHRISTIAN.] The troops have gone.

ROXANE. But the Cadets—Monsieur, you said ——

DE GUICHE. [*Sternly*] They go.
[*Draws paper from pocket.*]
Here is the order. [*To* CHRISTIAN.] Take it, Baron.

CHRISTIAN. [*Hesitating and bewildered*] But ——

ROXANE. [*Throwing herself into* CHRISTIAN'S *arms*] Christian!

DE GUICHE. [*Sneeringly*] The bridal night is still far off.

CHRISTIAN. [*To* ROXANE] Another kiss ——

CYRANO. Come, come—that is enough.

CHRISTIAN. You do not know how hard it is ——

CYRANO. I know.

DE GUICHE. [*Who has retired to the background*] The regiment is off.

ROXANE. [*To* CYRANO] Take care of him.
Never let him go where there is danger.

CYRANO. I'll try—but cannot promise.

ROXANE. Make him be careful.

CYRANO. I'll try, but ——

ROXANE. Keep him warm.

CYRANO. I'll do my best.

ROXANE. Oh—see that he is true to me ——

CYRANO. Of course.

ROXANE. And that he writes a letter often ——

CYRANO. That
I promise you.

[*There is a roll of drums in the distance.* ROXANE *sinks weeping into the arms of the* DUENNA.]

CURTAIN

ACT IV

SCENE: *A camp near Arras. In the back, a rocky rampart crossing the entire stage. Down* L., *a camp-fire.* CADETS *lie asleep, wrapped in their cloaks. The* CAPTAIN *and* LE BRET *are on guard. They are pale and thin. It is dawn, and gradually gets lighter as act advances. A* SENTINEL *stands on rock at rear, holding a lance.*

CAPTAIN. Frightful!
LE BRET. Yes, frightful.
CAPTAIN. Dieu! Trapped and starved.
LE BRET. Mordieu! [*He walks back and forth as if looking for someone.*]
CAPTAIN. Swear quietly. [*A few heads are raised.*]
Hush—go to sleep—
Who sleeps—dines. [*Shots in distance.*]
Diable! They'll wake my little ones.
Sleep on ——

[*Shots. Heads are raised.*]

FIRST CADET. Again.
SECOND CADET. Diable!
CAPTAIN. It is nothing—
Cyrano returns.

[CYRANO *comes over rampart.*]

LE BRET. De Bergerac—[*Goes to meet him.*]
Thank God!—Wounded?
CYRANO. [*Laughs*] No—each day they fire
And miss. It has become a habit. [*Laughs and goes to fire.*]

LE BRET. Fool!
To take a risk each day to send a letter.
CYRANO. [*Shrugs*] I gave my word that he would write to her ——
LE BRET. But—to risk your life! It is too much.
CYRANO.
Stop grumbling, friend. I'm safe enough.—Ah, Christian—
[*He looks down at* CHRISTIAN, *lying asleep.*]
Pale, but always good to look upon.
If she, poor little girl, knew he was starving ——
LE BRET. To risk your life!
CYRANO. Don't scold; [*his tone makes* LE BRET *look up*] we'll soon have news.
LE BRET. News?
CYRANO. [*Nods*] We either eat or die—to-night.
LE BRET. Tell on.
CYRANO. No—I'm not sure. We'll see ——
LE BRET. To-night ——
CAPTAIN.
To die of hunger while one lays a siege
Is sorry warfare.
CYRANO. [*Shrugs*] Such are the fortunes of war.
LE BRET.
And every day you risk a life like yours
Merely for ——
CYRANO. A letter—yes. [*Crosses* R. *toward his tent.*]
LE BRET. And now ——?
CYRANO. I go to write another.

[*Bugle is heard in distance.*] (*Bugle.*)

CAPTAIN. The reveille—alas ——

[CADETS *move.*]

FIRST CADET. I'm famished.

SECOND CADET. I believe I'm dying —— [*Tries to get up; sinks back.*]

ALL. Oh ——

CAPTAIN. Get up ——

THIRD CADET. I can't go a step.

FOURTH CADET. I'm starved.

FIFTH CADET. I haven't the strength to stir. My tongue is coated ——

SIXTH CADET. It must be the air that's indigestible.

SEVENTH CADET. My barony for a bit of Cheshire cheese.

CAPTAIN. [*Going to* CYRANO] Pluck up their spirits.

FIRST CADET. [*Falling on one that is chewing*] What are you eating, man?

SECOND CADET. A bit of gun tow fried in axle grease.

[*Two more* CADETS *enter.*]

EIGHTH CADET. I have been hunting ——

NINTH CADET. And I have caught a fish.

ALL. [*Getting up quickly*] What did you catch?—A pheasant?—A carp?—Quick ——

EIGHTH CADET. Alas—a sparrow.

NINTH CADET. And I—a minnow —— [*Groans.*]

ALL. We can't stand this.—We've had enough.—Bread! [*Grumbling.*]

CAPTAIN. Help, Cyrano—this may be mutiny.

CYRANO. [*Comes back on stage*] You there, why do you walk with lagging step?

FIRST CADET. I've something on my heels that troubles me.

CYRANO. And what is that?

FIRST CADET. My stomach.

CYRANO. So have I. [*Tightens belt.*]

FIRST CADET. Does it not trouble you?
CYRANO. It keeps me young.
SECOND CADET.
The Cardinal at home has four good meals
A day.
CYRANO. He really ought to send a partridge.
THIRD CADET. And wine.
CYRANO. Some Burgundy, Monseigneur, please?
Thank you.

[*Murmurs from* CADETS.]

FOURTH CADET. My teeth feel long.
CYRANO. The better to bite with.
FIFTH CADET. My stomach is as hollow as a drum.
CYRANO. We'll use it, then, to sound the charge——
FIFTH CADET. Bah—
Always a clever answer, and a jest.
CYRANO.
Aye—a jest—an answer to the point.
'Tis so I hope to die 'neath rose-flushed skies
For a good cause. Or else in combat with
A worthy foe to fall on field of honor—
Steel in my heart—and on my lips—a laugh.
SIXTH CADET.
H'm.—This is no time for cleverness
Or dreams.
ALL. We're hungry.
CYRANO. Bah.—You think of naught
But food. Come, Bertrando—you were a shepherd
Once—in Gascony. Take out your fife
And blow upon it to this lazy pack
Of gluttons songs of home that hold us fast;
In which each note is like a little sister,

Airs sweet and slow, old southern melodies
That bring back Gascon skies to smile on us,
Soft Gascon winds and Gascon voices that
We love.

(*Flute Solo Softly.*)

[BERTRANDO *begins to play. Gradually, the restless* CADETS *settle down and listen.*]

List, Gascons! For now we hear no more
The camp's shrill fife, but the soft woodland flute—
No more the battle blast—but goatherd's pipe,
Sweet, quiet, cool—and singing plaintively
Of forest, vale and plain; of the Dordoyne
And its long evenings green and cool, and filled
With peace. List, Gascons—it is all Gascony.

[*As the shepherd plays, every head is bowed, and here and there a tear is wiped away.*]

(*Music stops.*)

CAPTAIN. You make them weep ——

CYRANO. With homesickness—a pain
That's nobler far than hunger.

SENTRY. [*From rampart*] Vicomte de Guiche.

CADETS. [*Derisively as* DE GUICHE *enters*] Hoo! Hoo!

CAPTAIN. He has a hungry look—like us.

LE BRET. And proud ——

CYRANO. [*To* CADETS]
Your cards—your pipes. We'll not appear
To suffer either. I will read Descartes.

[*All hurriedly find something to do. When* DE GUICHE *comes down, all are busy and seem contented.*]

DE GUICHE.
Good day.—Are these the malcontents?—I hear
I am lampooned on every side, and that,
In short, you cannot find hard words enough
For your commander; that it troubles you
To see a point-lace collar on my cuirass;
And that you never cease to take it ill
That every Gascon need not be a beggar.
[*They play and smoke.*]
Shall I, then, have you punished by your captain?

CAPTAIN. I am free and give no punishment.

DE GUICHE. Ah!

CAPTAIN. I've paid my company; it is my own.

DE GUICHE.
Indeed! Your mockery I despise. You know
How I stand fire—and how I put to flight
The Count of Bucquoi. Like an avalanche
I hurled my men on his—thrice and again
I charged ——

CYRANO. And your white scarf?

DE GUICHE. You know? Pressed hard
By foes, I had wit enough to drop to earth
The scarf that showed my rank and so escape
The Spaniards and return incognito—[*Proudly*]
To lead my rallied force and win the fight.
What say you of this feat?

CYRANO. That Henri quatre
Would never have agreed 'gainst any odds
To take one feather from his snow white crest.

[*Silent joy on part of all* CADETS. *Cards are let fall.*]

DE GUICHE. [*With assurance*] But still the ruse succeeded!

CYRANO. Lend it to me,
And on this very night I'll lead the assault,
The white scarf draped about me.

DE GUICHE. Boasting still?
Gascon braggart—you know well the scarf
Was lost within the foemen's lines. No one
Would dare to seek it.

[CYRANO *takes scarf from pocket and returns it to* DE GUICHE. CADETS *smother their laughter, whistle, grow serious as* DE GUICHE *looks at them.*]

CYRANO. Here it is.

DE GUICHE. [*Taking scarf*] Good.
With this I'll wave the signal I was loath
To give. [*He goes to rampart and waves scarf several times.*]

CADETS. Who's there?

DE GUICHE. Apparently, a spy
Who serves the foe: in truth, the instrument
By which, unknown to them, I shape their plans.

CADETS. [*Murmuring*] A scurvy trick.

DE GUICHE. Perhaps—but—[*shrugs*] it works.
And to resume—I came to tell you news—
A desperate stroke to obtain supplies.

CADETS. [*Joyfully*] Supplies!

DE GUICHE. [*Nods*]
The Marshal goes to Dourlens, without drums;
The King's provision trains are there. But to
Get back with ease, he's taken half our force.

CAPTAIN. The Spaniards do not know?

DE GUICHE. They know.

CADETS. They know?

CAPTAIN. Ah!

DE GUICHE.
My spy will tell them where to attack—
[*There is a silence.*]
'Twill be the spot where I just gave the signal.
CAPTAIN. Make ready, gentlemen ——

[*All rise, buckle belts, fix swords.*]

DE GUICHE. 'Tis in an hour—
[*All sit down again.*]
You must gain time. The Marshal will return ——
CADETS. And to gain time ——?
DE GUICHE. You'll kindly give your lives.
CAPTAIN. Ah! [*He looks at* CADETS *who maintain absolute silence.*]
CYRANO. And so—Monsieur—you take your vengeance.
DE GUICHE. [*Shrugs*]
Had I been fond of you, perhaps I might
Have spared you this—but since none vie with you
In reckless daring, I do two things at once—
I serve my King and satisfy my grudge.
CYRANO.
Permit me, sir, to express my gratitude.
[*To the* CADETS.]
My friends—we'll add to the Gascon crest—which now
Six chevrons bears—of azure and of gold—
One chevron more—blood red —— [*He goes to* CHRISTIAN.] Christian!

[*They go to fire.*]

CHRISTIAN. Roxane!
CYRANO. Alas ——

CHRISTIAN. That I might write one last farewell ——

CYRANO.

You have—I had no doubt the end was near,
And I have written your farewell for you.

CHRISTIAN. Show it.

CYRANO. Do you wish ——? [*Takes letter from his doublet.*]

CHRISTIAN. Why, yes.—[*Opens it, reads.* CYRANO *walks away.* CHRISTIAN *stops suddenly.*] But this ——?

CYRANO. What?

CHRISTIAN. This little spot —— [*Goes over to* CYRANO R. C.]

CYRANO. A spot?

CHRISTIAN. A tear.

CYRANO.

Why, so it is—this very morning—this—
This little note—it made me weep ——

CHRISTIAN. You wept?—
Because ——

CYRANO. Why, yes. To die is nothing much—
But ne'er again to see her—I—[CHRISTIAN *looks at him sharply*] we ——

CHRISTIAN. Give me the letter.

[*Shots are heard. All hurry to rampart.*]

SENTRY. Halt there! Who goes there?

[*Shots, voices.*]

CAPTAIN. What is it?

SENTRY. A coach!

CADETS. What—here in the camp?
It enters!—It comes from the enemy! Fire!—

No!—The driver shouts—shouts what?—He shouts,
"On the King's service!"

[*Everyone is on the rampart.*]

DE GUICHE. What—the King?

[*The* CADETS *come down.*]

CAPTAIN. Hats off!
DE GUICHE.
From the King! Take your places, wretched rabble!
That he may enter in befitting state.
CAPTAIN. Fall in!

[CADETS *line up.*]

CYRANO. The coach stops.—Mon dieu!

[*He rushes to* CHRISTIAN *and they stand in excited conference when* ROXANE *enters and makes an elaborate bow.*]

ROXANE. Good-morning.

[*The sound of a woman's voice brings on blank amazement.*]

DE GUICHE. On the King's service—you?
ROXANE. My own King—Love!
CYRANO. Mon dieu!
CHRISTIAN. [*Rushing forward*] You!—Why ——!
ROXANE. This siege was far too long.
CHRISTIAN. Why?
ROXANE. I'll tell you.

[CYRANO, *at the sound of her voice, has remained mo-*

tionless, rooted to the spot, not daring to look at her.]

DE GUICHE. You cannot stay here.

ROXANE. [*Gaily*]
Oh, yes I can. Will you hand me a drum?
[*She sits down on the drum that is handed to her.*]
There—many thanks! They fired on us—[*proudly*] a patrol!
[*She throws a kiss to* CHRISTIAN.]
Good-morning. You do not look gay, Messieurs.
You know 'tis far to Arras? [*Sees* CYRANO.] Cousin, I'm charmed.

CYRANO. But how, Madame——?

ROXANE. Heavens, my friend, 'twas simple.

CYRANO. But this is mad—where did you pass?

ROXANE. Where?
Through the Spanish lines.

[CADETS *murmur.*]

FIRST CADET. An evil lot.

DE GUICHE. But how did you contrive to pass their lines?

LE BRET. It must have been no easy task——

ROXANE. Why, yes—
I simply sent my carriage at full speed:
If a hidalgo showed an arrogant air,
I merely beamed on him my sweetest smile——

CAPTAIN.
Yes, 'tis a passport sure, that smile of yours.
But still they often must have asked of you
Whither you went at such a pace, Madame?

ROXANE.
They often did; and then I always answered,
"I go to see my lover!" Then the Spaniard
E'en of the fiercest air, would gravely close
My carriage door, and with a courtly gesture
The King himself would envy, wave away
The guns already leveled at my breast:
And gorgeous in his grace and in his pride,
He would bow low and say, "Pass, Señorita!"

CHRISTIAN. But ——

ROXANE.
I said, "My lover," yes: but, pardon—
You understand, if I had said, "My husband,"
None would have let me pass.

CHRISTIAN. But ——

ROXANE. What's the matter?

DE GUICHE. You must depart.

ROXANE. I?

CYRANO. Quickly.

LE BRET. Yes, at once!

CHRISTIAN. Yes ——

ROXANE. Why?

CHRISTIAN. [*Embarrassed*] The fact is ——

CYRANO. [*In the same tone*] In the next half hour ——

DE GUICHE. [*Same tone*] About ——

CAPTAIN. [*Same tone*] 'Tis better ——

LE BRET. [*Same tone*] You might ——

ROXANE. I shall stay.
A battle's near!

ALL. Oh, no!

ROXANE. [*Throws herself in* CHRISTIAN's *arms*]
This is my husband!
Let me be slain with him.

DE GUICHE. The danger's great ——
ROXANE. Great? The danger's great?
LE BRET. [*Looking at* DE GUICHE] He made it so ——
ROXANE. Ah, then you wish me widowed.
DE GUICHE. No—I swear ——
ROXANE. Well, I am a little mad just now. I stay.
CADETS. She stays!
CYRANO. What! Has Madame become a heroine?
ROXANE. Monsieur de Bergerac, I am your cousin ——
FIRST CADET. We will defend you.
ROXANE. Friends, that I believe.
SECOND CADET. The whole camp smells of iris.
ROXANE. I have on
A hat which will look very well in battle.
[*Looks at* DE GUICHE.]
Perhaps 'tis time the Count should go away—
They might begin!

[CADETS *laugh.*]

DE GUICHE. This is too much. I go—
But will return at once. Pray change your mind.
ROXANE. No—never.

[*Exit* DE GUICHE.]

CHRISTIAN. But, Roxane ——
ROXANE. No!
FIRST CADET. She will stay!

[*All rush about to make themselves presentable.*]

ALL. A comb—a brush—some soap—my clothes are torn—
Give me a needle—a ribbon—here, your mirror—
My gauntlets—curling irons—a razor—quick!

ROXANE. [*To* CHRISTIAN] No—naught shall make me stir out of this place.

CAPTAIN. [*After having, like the rest, tightened his belt, brushed his clothes, etc., advances toward* ROXANE]

Madame, may I present these gentlemen
Who'll have the honor to die before your eyes?

[ROXANE *bows and waits on* CHRISTIAN'S *arm. The* CADETS *stand in line.*]

These are the Cadets of Gascony—
Carbon de Castel-Jaloux's men—Madame
Roxane Robin—de Neuvillette ——

[*Instead of saluting, they bow.* ROXANE *curtseys deeply, drops her handkerchief, they all rush forward, but the* CAPTAIN *seizes it and fixes it on his lance.*]

May I,
Madame?

ROXANE. 'Tis rather small ——

CAPTAIN. But all of lace—
The finest standard in the camp.

CADETS. Bravo!

FIRST CADET.
I should die gladly now—if only first
I might have one small bite to eat.

CAPTAIN. But shame!

ROXANE.
Nay—I am hungry, too. Pasties and game
And wine—that is my choice. Will you bring them,
Please?

SECOND CADET. [*In consternation*] All?

THIRD CADET. Where shall we get them?

ROXANE. In my coach.

ALL. What?

[RAGUENEAU *approaches with a hamper.*]

ROXANE. [*Introducing him*] My coachman, sirs,—a genius ——

ALL. Why—
'Tis Ragueneau—oh—oh ——

ROXANE. Poor boys ——

CYRANO. [*Kissing her hand*] Good fairy ——

RAGUENEAU. Gentlemen,—come. [*He leads the way to the coach.*]

CADETS. [*Following*] Bravo!—Bravo!—Bravo!

[*All go except* ROXANE, CYRANO *and* CHRISTIAN. CHRISTIAN *takes* ROXANE *in his arms and* CYRANO *goes aside, frowning.*]

DE GUICHE. [*Enters hastily*] Madame, have you decided?

ROXANE. I stay here.

DE GUICHE. 'Tis certain death ——

ROXANE. I stay ——

DE GUICHE. Then I stay, too.

CYRANO. Sir, you show courage ——

[CADETS *have come in and listened.*]

CAPTAIN. You are a Gascon,
Then, despite your lace?

DE GUICHE. I do not leave
A woman in distress.

FIRST CADET. Really,—I think
We well might give him food.

DE GUICHE. Food!
[*Each* CADET *offers him some food he has been hiding.*]

Do you, then,
Think that I will eat your leavings?

CYRANO. You
Are making progress now ——

DE GUICHE. [*Proudly*] I shall fight fasting.

FIRST CADET. There spoke a Gascon.

DE GUICHE. I?

SECOND CADET. He's one of us!

[*All salute him as the* CAPTAIN *reappears from behind the rampart.*]

CAPTAIN. I've placed my lancers there in open order. [*Points.*]

DE GUICHE. [*Bowing to* ROXANE] Will you accept my arm for the review?

[*She accepts, and they go toward the rampart. Everyone uncovers and follows them.* CHRISTIAN *goes quickly to* CYRANO.]

CHRISTIAN. Speak, quick.—What was the secret?

[ROXANE *reaches the rampart. The rest go on past her. She waves. They shout from the distance. She stands very still.*]

CADETS. Hurrah! Hurrah!

[*She waves.*]

CYRANO. If perchance Roxane ——

CHRISTIAN. Well?

CYRANO. Should speak to you
Of letters ——

CHRISTIAN. Oh, I know!

CYRANO. Have not the folly
To show surprise.

CHRISTIAN. At what?

CYRANO. Well, I must tell you—
I've written oftener than you think..

CHRISTIAN. How's that?
How many times, then, have you passed the lines
At peril of your life? Two—three—or four?

CYRANO. Oftener ——

CHRISTIAN. Every day?

CYRANO. Yes—twice a day.

[*The shouts have died away, and* ROXANE *comes down.*]

ROXANE. And now, Christian—not a word?

[CYRANO *walks away.*]

CHRISTIAN. Roxane—
Now tell me why you came to join me here.

ROXANE. It was your letters.

CHRISTIAN. What?

ROXANE. Yes, your letters
Turned my head. Every one was better
Than the last ——

CHRISTIAN. My letters brought you here?

ROXANE.
I've worshiped you since on that night you spoke
Beneath my window—with a voice whose tones
I had not heard before—and that revealed
Your soul: for had Ulysses written words
Like yours, Penelope would ne'er have stayed
At home, but gone to seek her husband.

CHRISTIAN. But ——

ROXANE.
I read, and read again—I felt your love—
So strong and so sincere ——

CHRISTIAN. So strong—sincere—
You felt it there, Roxane?

ROXANE. Indeed I did.

CHRISTIAN. And you have come ——

ROXANE. Oh, Christian, oh, my love,
I come to crave your pardon—for having loved
At first only your comeliness.

CHRISTIAN. [*In alarm*] Roxane!

ROXANE. But soon—dear love—I loved you for your soul.

CHRISTIAN. [*Sadly*] Roxane ——

ROXANE. You do not see?—I'd love you still
If you should lose all comeliness at once.

CHRISTIAN. Oh, say not so ——

ROXANE. 'Tis what I mean!

CHRISTIAN. What!—Ugly?

ROXANE. Ugly—I swear it!

CHRISTIAN. Dieu!

ROXANE. Your joy is deep?

CHRISTIAN. [*In smothered voice*] Yes ——

ROXANE. But ——

CHRISTIAN. [*Pointing to* CADETS *in background*] Go smile on them before they die ——

ROXANE. [*Much moved*] Dear Christian —— [*She goes to* CADETS, *who crowd around her.*]

CHRISTIAN. Cyrano!

CYRANO. [*Coming from* R., *armed for battle*] What—pale?—Is she ——

CHRISTIAN. No longer does she love me!

CYRANO. What?

CHRISTIAN. 'Tis you!

CYRANO. No!

CHRISTIAN. 'Tis my soul she loves:—you love her, too!

CYRANO. I?

CHRISTIAN. I know it!

CYRANO. It is true.

CHRISTIAN. Madly!

CYRANO. Yes, more!

CHRISTIAN. Tell her ——

CYRANO. No!

CHRISTIAN. But why not?

CYRANO. Look at my face!

CHRISTIAN. She would love me—ugly.

CYRANO. Did she say so?

CHRISTIAN. Yes ——

CYRANO. Ah—I'm glad she did—
But do not take her at her word.

CHRISTIAN. I must—
And she must choose; for you shall tell her all.
I'm weary of this rival in myself.

CYRANO. Christian!

CHRISTIAN. Our union—secret—all unknown—
Can be annulled—if we survive. Speak—
And let her choose between us.

CYRANO. No!—

CHRISTIAN. [*Firmly*] I'll go
To see what is on foot. When I return—
I'll know.

CYRANO. It will be you.

CHRISTIAN. Dear God—I pray —— [*Turns quickly away and calls.*] Roxane!

ROXANE. What is it?

CHRISTIAN. Cyrano has news ——
Important news. [*He exits.*]

ROXANE. Important?

CYRANO. He has gone ——

ROXANE. [*Puzzled*] But ——

CYRANO. It is nothing.—He makes much of little.
You should know him better by this time.

ROXANE,
He did not believe what I just said—
I saw he had his doubts.

CYRANO. [*Taking her hand*] But what you told
Him was the truth?

ROXANE. Yes ——

CYRANO. You told him ——

ROXANE. That I
Should love him—even if —— [*She hesitates.*]

CYRANO. You hesitate
To say the word to me?

ROXANE. But ——

CYRANO. If he were ugly ——?

ROXANE. Yes. [*A shot off stage.*] A shot!

CYRANO. Hideous?

ROXANE. Yes.

CYRANO. Disfigured?

ROXANE. Yes.

CYRANO. Grotesque?

ROXANE. Nothing could make him that
To me.

CYRANO. You still would love him?

ROXANE. Yes—and more.

CYRANO.
My God—perhaps 'tis true. Bliss—at last ——
[*Then to* ROXANE.]
Roxane—listen —— [*Takes her hand.*]

LE BRET. [*Enters and speaks softly*] Cyrano ——

CYRANO. What?
LE BRET. [*Whispers in his ear, then*] Hush!
CYRANO. Ah! [*He drops* ROXANE's *hand with a cry.*]
ROXANE. What's the matter?

[*Shots off stage. She goes toward rampart.* LE BRET *detains her while* CHRISTIAN, *wounded, is carried in* R.]

CYRANO. [*To himself*] It is done. [*Two shots.*] They fire!
ROXANE. What now?

[LE BRET *keeps her attention centered back* L.]

CYRANO. [*Pushing aside one of the* CADETS, *puts his arm around* CHRISTIAN] 'Tis *you* she loves ——!
CHRISTIAN. [*Raising his head, gasps*] Ah —— [*Dies.*]
CYRANO. It is done—
Now I can never tell her ——

[CADETS *stand around* CHRISTIAN *down* R. C., *hiding him from view.* ROXANE *turns.*]

ROXANE. What is this?
What's going on?—These men ——?
CYRANO. [*Going up to her*] Nothing—I swear
That Christian's spirit and Christian's soul
Were ——
ROXANE. Were ——? [*With a cry.*] Oh! [*She rushes toward the body.*]
CYRANO. It is done!
ROXANE. Christian, my love. [*She throws herself on the body. More shots off stage.*]
LE BRET. The foe's first fire. [*Shots.*]

CAPTAIN. 'Tis the attack! To arms!

[*Followed by* CADETS *he dashes over rampart. Firing and shouts continue.* CYRANO *remains with* ROXANE.]

ROXANE.

Is he dead? [*Shouts.*] I feel his cheek grow cold
'Gainst mine.
[*She opens his coat to feel his heart.*]
A letter.—'Tis for me.

CYRANO. Roxane—
I go—I must—the fight is on.

ROXANE. Stay yet
A while.—He's dead.—You were his friend. Was he
Not wonderful, my Christian?

CYRANO. Yes, Roxane ——

ROXANE. A poet to adore?

CYRANO. Yes, Roxane ——

ROXANE. A lofty spirit?

CYRANO. Yes ——

ROXANE. A mighty heart ——
Undreamt of by the crowd — a glorious soul ——?

CYRANO. Yes, Roxane ——

[*Shots continue from here to the end.*]

ROXANE. [*Weeping*] He died ——

CYRANO. [*Aside*] And only death
Is left for me.

[ROXANE *weeps over the body.* DE GUICHE *comes in wounded.* CYRANO *indicates in pantomime that he shall take care of* ROXANE. *There are cries, shots;* CYRANO *rushes to rampart, draws sword.*] "Ce sont les Cadets de Gascogne de Carbon de Castel Jaloux ——" [*He fights with someone beyond and below the rampart, amid shots and clashing of sabres.*]

CURTAIN

ACT V

(*Chime on upper Pin Rail strikes Four, just before Curtain opens.*)

SCENE: (*Fifteen years later.*) *The garden of the convent of the Sisters of the Cross in Paris.* L., *the convent chapel;* L. C., *a bench;* R., *a large tree. It is autumn, and leaves fall during entire scene. It is late afternoon, very gradually darkening to twilight. Nuns are busy with handwork.*

SISTER MARTHA. [*To* MOTHER MARGARET]
Sister Clair looked in the glass—twice—
At her new cap.
MOTHER MARGARET. But it is very ugly.
SISTER CLAIR.
And I saw Sister Martha steal a plum
Out of the tart this morning.
MOTHER MARGARET. That was wrong,
Very wrong.
SISTER CLAIR. But such a little look ——
SISTER MARTHA. And such a little plum ——
MOTHER MARGARET. I shall tell
Monsieur de Bergerac this evening.
SISTER CLAIR. Oh, please, he will make fun of us.
SISTER MARTHA. He'll say
That nuns are very vain ——
SISTER CLAIR. And greedy ——
MOTHER MARGARET. [*Smiling*] Yes—
And very good.
SISTER CLAIR. But, Mother, is't not so
That he has come each Saturday these ten
Years past?

MOTHER MARGARET.
Even longer. Ever since his cousin
Came here to live with us—her coif of black
Among our sober linen robes—like some
Great black-plumed bird among gray doves.—
Yes,
That was fourteen years ago.
SISTER MARTHA. Her sorrow
Seems somehow her dearest joy. [*Sighs.*]—He
Alone can make her smile.
SISTER CLAIR. He is such fun—
It's cheerful when he comes.—He teases us.
We love him, don't we? He is so kind—
He likes our candied fruit cake—too.
SISTER MARTHA. I fear,
Though, that he is not a good Catholic.
SISTER CLAIR. We will convert him ——
SISTERS. Yes ——
MOTHER MARGARET. No—let him be—
I will not have you worry him. He may—
Come less—perchance ——
SISTER MARTHA. But God ——
MOTHER MARGARET. Be not disturbed.
God knows him well.
SISTER MARTHA. Ye-es, Mother,—but yet—
Each Saturday when he comes, he says to me—
And proudly, too—" I ate meat yesterday."
MOTHER MARGARET.
He tells you that? The last time that he came,
He had eaten nothing for two whole days.
SISTER MARTHA. Mother!
MOTHER MARGARET. He is poor—very poor.
SISTER MARTHA. Who told you?
MOTHER MARGARET. Monsieur Le Bret.

SISTER MARTHA. Does no one help him?

MOTHER MARGARET.
No—that would anger him—for he is proud—
Very proud ——

[*In the background,* ROXANE *appears, dressed in black with a widow's cap and veil.* DE GUICHE, *very elegant, but growing old, walks near her. They approach slowly.* MOTHER MARGARET *rises.*]

SISTER MARTHA. But, Mother ——

MOTHER MARGARET. Let us go in. [*They look at her in surprise, then notice* ROXANE *and* DE GUICHE.] Madame Madeleine has a visitor ——

SISTER MARTHA. [*To* SISTER CLAIR] The Duc de Grammont?

SISTER CLAIR. Yes, I think it is.

SISTER MARTHA. He has not been to see her for many months.

SISTERS. He's busy—with the Court—the field ——

SISTER CLAIR. The world.

[*They exit.* DE GUICHE *and* ROXANE *come down in silence and stop near the bench.*]

DE GUICHE. So you dwell here—in mourning—always?

ROXANE. Always.

DE GUICHE. And faithful as of old?

ROXANE. Forever faithful ——

DE GUICHE. Have you forgiven me ——?

ROXANE. [*Looking up at convent*] I am here —— [*Silence.*]

DE GUICHE. So Christian was all that?

ROXANE. When you knew him.

DE GUICHE.
I did not know him well enough—perhaps.
And his last letter—always still against
Your heart?

ROXANE. A holy reliquary.

DE GUICHE. Dead—
And yet you love him ——

ROXANE. Yes—sometimes it seems
He is not dead; our hearts meet even now—
His love surrounds me always.

DE GUICHE. Ah—your cousin,
Monsieur de Bergerac comes yet?

ROXANE. Often—
This faithful friend is my gazette. He comes
Each Saturday afternoon—he never fails.
Whene'er the weather's fine they place his chair
Beneath that tree. I sit at my embroidery
And wait for him. The hour strikes—I listen—
With the last stroke I hear the tapping of
His cane upon the steps. I do not turn
To look, so well I know 'tis Cyrano.
He seats himself in his great chair and jests
At my eternal needlework—and then
He tells me all the news. [LE BRET *enters.*]
Ah—Monsieur Le Bret—
How does our friend?

LE BRET. Ill ——

ROXANE. [*Not anxiously*] Oh ——

DE GUICHE. Indeed!

ROXANE. Le Bret is overanxious ——

LE BRET. It is all
As I foretold.—Loneliness—poverty—
A host of enemies; and yet he hurls
His satires at all shams—sham noblemen—

Hypocrites—sham heroes—yes, sham artists,
Who flaunt the wit of others as their own—
In short, he hurls his shafts at all the world.

ROXANE. But still they fear his sword. No one dares touch him.

DE GUICHE. H'm—perhaps.

LE BRET. But what I fear for him
Is not fair open fight—[ROXANE *looks up*] 'tis solitude
And hunger—winter's cold, that enters his
Dark chamber on wolf's feet:—they are the swordsmen
That will vanquish him; for every day
He draws his belt in more—his poor great nose
Looks like old ivory—he has one coat—
A shabby old black serge ——

DE GUICHE. And yet, though he
Has not attained success, he has won that
Which is more rare—he does not need your pity.

LE BRET. [*Bitterly*] Monsieur le Duc!

DE GUICHE. I say he does not need
Your pity. For he has lived without concession—
Free in thought and deed.

LE BRET. My lord ——

DE GUICHE. I know
What you would say!—I've all things; he has nothing.
And yet I honor him and would be proud
To take his hand. [*To* ROXANE.]—Adieu.

ROXANE. I will go with you.

DE GUICHE. [*Continuing thoughtfully*]
Sometimes I envy him.—When life has brought
Too much success—too lightly won—one feels

Although one's done no downright wrong, God knows—
A thousand petty quarrels with one's self
Which all combined, together only make
A dull disgust with life—not quite remorse.
And while one mounts the steps of worldly power
And pomp—in the ermined mantle of a duke—
E'en that rich robe draws after it a host
Of dead illusions, vain regrets—as now
Your trailing gown draws up these convent stairs
The hollow whisper of seared autumn leaves.

ROXANE. [*Ironically*] You pensive—and regretful?

DE GUICHE. I?—Perhaps—[*Suddenly.*]
Monsieur Le Bret—[*to* ROXANE] you'll pardon me?—a word.
[*He approaches* LE BRET.]
'Tis true no one dares openly attack
Your friend, but many hate him heartily.
They told me at the Queen's the other day,
"This Cyrano may die—by accident."

LE BRET. Ah?

DE GUICHE. Yes. Keep him at home. He must be cautious.

LE BRET.
Cautious? Cyrano? He's coming here.
I'll warn him, but ——

[*A nun enters from convent* L.]

ROXANE. What is it, Sister?

SISTER. Ragueneau to see Madame ——

ROXANE. [*Nods*] He's come
For sympathy.

[RAGUENEAU *comes down convent steps.*]

RAGUENEAU. Madame——

ROXANE. There's Le Bret—
Tell him your troubles. I'll return. [*She turns and exits with* DE GUICHE.]

RAGUENEAU. [*Anxiously*] Madame—— [*Then to* LE BRET.]
Since you are here, 'tis best she should not know.
As I was on my way to see our friend,
And still some twenty paces from the door,
I saw him coming out. I went to meet him,
And as he turned the corner of the street,
From out a window under which he paused,
A lackey dropped a log of wood——

LE BRET. Cowards.

RAGUENEAU. Our friend, Monsieur, our noble poet——

LE BRET. Frightful.

RAGUENEAU. There on the ground—a great wound in his head.

LE BRET. He's dead?

RAGUENEAU. No, but—I bore him to his room—
Mon dieu!—His room! His wretched pallet—

LE BRET. But—
Is he suffering?

RAGUENEAU. No—unconscious——

LE BRET. Ah—
A doctor?

RAGUENEAU. Yes—one came—for charity.

LE BRET. [*Groans*]
Poor Cyrano. We'll break it to Roxane.
What did the doctor say?

RAGUENEAU. I hardly know.
Cerebral inflammation—fever—ah,
If you had seen him; his poor bandaged head.

Come quickly—there is no one at his side,
And if he rises—he will die.

LE BRET. [*Leading the way to* L.] This way,
'Tis shorter through the chapel.

ROXANE. [*Returning* R., *sees them hurrying out*]
Monsieur Le Bret —— [*He does not answer.*]
They run away. Poor Ragueneau's in trouble
Once again. September! What a day!
Autumn burnishes the gloom of sorrow—
On such a day my sadness seems almost
To smile.—Here comes the classic chair in which
My old friend always sits.

[*Nuns carry chair to tree* R.]

SISTER MARTHA. The best we have
In the convent parlor.

ROXANE. Thank you, Sister. [*Clock strikes five.*]

(*Chime on upper Pin Rail.*)

There!
The hour.—Now he will come.—My embroidery—
[*Chimes stop striking. She listens and frowns.*]
I am amazed. Will he for once be late?
The Sister at the gate—where is my thimble?—
Must be exhorting him to penitence.—
I've found it now.—She is exhorting him.
He cannot tarry long. A fallen leaf—
[*She brushes it away.*]
Besides nothing could keep him.—Now, my scissors—
Here in my bag ——

SISTER. [*Appears on the steps*] Monsieur de Bergerac ——

ROXANE. [*Without turning*] What was I saying?—Ah—these faded colors! [*To* CYRANO, *in tones of friendly scolding.*] Late, cousin—the first time in fourteen years.

CYRANO. [*Sitting down in the armchair and speaking in a cheerful voice in contrast to his expression*]
Yes. 'Tis absurd. I was beside myself—
I was detained.

ROXANE. Detained?

CYRANO. A visitor—
Most unexpected.

ROXANE. Some troublesome fellow?

CYRANO. Well—inopportune.

ROXANE. You excused yourself?

CYRANO.
For a while—yes. I said, "You'll pardon me—
But this is Saturday, and rain or shine
I must betake me to a certain house
To pay a visit there. So come again—
Within an hour ——"

ROXANE. This friend of yours must wait.
I shall not let you go till evening.

CYRANO. Perhaps a little sooner—I must go ——
[*He leans back wearily.*]

[SISTER MARTHA *enters and stands some distance behind his chair.*]

ROXANE. Someone is waiting to be teased.

CYRANO. Aha—
Sister, come here. Beautiful, downcast eyes
Always studying the ground.

SISTER MARTHA. [*Lifts her eyes and notices his pallor*] But —— Oh!

CYRANO. [*Indicating* ROXANE] Hush!
'Tis nothing—yesterday I ate meat again!

SISTER MARTHA.
I understand. That's why he is so pale!
Come to the refectory—I'll make
A fine big bowl of broth. You'll come, Monsieur?

CYRANO. Come?

SISTER MARTHA. You are quite reasonable to-day.

ROXANE. Is she trying to convert you?

SISTER MARTHA. No—no—
Not for the world ——

CYRANO. What? You who are so good,
Not trying to make me good also? Astonishing!
But now—I shall astonish you.—To-night
At vespers you shall pray for me.

ROXANE. Aha ——

CYRANO. Look at her—dumb with astonishment.

SISTER MARTHA. [*Softly*] I did not wait for your permission —— [*Exits.*]

CYRANO. H'm—[*Turning to* ROXANE.]
The devil take me, but shall I never see
An end to this eternal needlework?

ROXANE. I thought 'twas time you made that jest.

CYRANO. The leaves—

ROXANE. Perfect Venetian gold. See how they fall ——

CYRANO.
Ah, they know how to die. How gracefully
In that last journey do they fall from branch
To earth, putting on, as 'twere, a final
Fleeting charm, as if, though loath to molder

In the common dust, they would go down
In beauty, giving to their fall the grace
Of flight.

ROXANE. You—melancholy?

CYRANO. No, Roxane ——

ROXANE.
Then let the leaves fall as they will. I wait
To hear the news from my gazette.

CYRANO. Ah, yes,
The news. Well, let me see. On Saturday,
The nineteenth—his Majesty the King was ill.
Too many helpings of his favorite sweets,
'Tis said—brought on the fever. He was bled—
His illness was found guilty of high treason,
And now his august pulse is calm again.
On Sunday, at the Queen's grand ball, they burned
Seven hundred sixty-three wax candles.
They say our troops have been victorious
In Austria. But more important far—
The little dog of Madame d'Athis was ill—
The doctor ordered pills ——

ROXANE. Monsieur de Bergerac ——

CYRANO. Nothing on Monday—but Lygdamire's new lover.

ROXANE. Ah ——

CYRANO. Tuesday, the whole court went to Fontainebleau.
Wednesday, de Fiesque had "No" from La Montglat.
Thursday, Masscini is Queen of France—almost!
Friday, La Montglat said "Yes," and on
The twenty-sixth—on Saturday ——

[*His eyes close, his head droops;—silence.* ROXANE, *surprised, turns, looks at him, and gets up in fright.*]

ROXANE. He's fainted.
Cousin—Cyrano—what is it? What?
He's fainted! [*Rushes to him.*]—Cyrano ——

CYRANO. What is it?—What?—
[*He sees* ROXANE *leaning over him, quickly settles his hat on his head and draws back in alarm.*]
No—no—'tis nothing—let me be!

ROXANE. But ——

CYRANO. 'Tis my wound from Arras which at times,
You know ——

ROXANE. Poor friend ——

CYRANO. 'Tis naught—'twill pass—[*smiles with effort*] has passed ——

ROXANE.
We all have our old wounds. I, too, have mine;
My old wound—one that never heals—here.
[*Lays hand on her breast.*]
Here 'neath this faded letter with its blood
And tears ——

[*Twilight has been falling.*]

CYRANO. His letter—did you not promise
To let me read it sometime ——?

ROXANE. His letter?—
You wish to read ——?

CYRANO. [*Nods*] To-day—it is my wish —— [*Holds out his hand.*]

ROXANE. [*Hesitates, then gives him the letter*] Here.

CYRANO. I may open?

ROXANE. Open—read —— [*She returns to her work.*]

CYRANO. [*Reading*] Farewell—
Roxane,—to-night I die ——

ROXANE. You read aloud?

CYRANO.
Roxane, my own beloved—my soul to-night
Is heavy with love I have not told you;
And now I die and you will never know;
And never more will my enraptured eyes ——

ROXANE. How you read his letter ——

CYRANO. Behold the grace—
The charming grace of you ——

ROXANE. His letter—how
You read it!

[*Night is falling imperceptibly.*]

CYRANO. I would fain cry out ——

ROXANE. You read ——

CYRANO. Farewell, my heart's dearest ——

ROXANE. With a voice ——

CYRANO. My best beloved ——

ROXANE. That I have heard before! [*She goes softly behind his chair without his noticing, leans over and looks at the letter. Darkness is deepening.*]

CYRANO.
I am always with you, and even now
I shall not leave you. In that other world
I shall be he who loves you beyond measure,
He who ——

ROXANE. But it is dark.—How can you read?
[*He starts, turns, bows his head.*]
How can you?—And all these fourteen years
He's been the friend who came to be amusing.

CYRANO. Roxane ——

ROXANE. It was you ——

CYRANO. No—no—Roxane ——

ROXANE. I should have guessed it when he spoke my name ——

CYRANO. No—no—it was not I ——

ROXANE. It was you ——

CYRANO. I swear ——

ROXANE.

At last I see it all.—The letters—they
Were yours ——

CYRANO. No—no ——

ROXANE. The dear, mad words—were yours ——

CYRANO. No ——

ROXANE. The voice in the night was yours ——

CYRANO. I swear—
It was not ——

ROXANE. The soul—that was yours.

CYRANO. I never loved you ——

ROXANE. You loved me ——

CYRANO. It was he ——

ROXANE. You loved me ——

CYRANO. [*Softly*] No ——

ROXANE. [*Smiling sadly*] How faintly you deny ——

CYRANO. No—no—my dearest love—I never loved you ——

ROXANE.

Alas—how many things have died and are
New born. Why have you been silent—all
These fourteen years? This letter—and the tears—
Were yours ——

CYRANO. The blood—was his ——

ROXANE. And why did you
Decide to break this silence now—to-day?

CYRANO. Why?

[LE BRET *and* RAGUENEAU *enter, running.*]

LE BRET. What madness —— [*Sees* CYRANO.] I knew it. There he is.

CYRANO. [*Straightening and smiling*] Well!—Here I am!

RAGUENEAU. [*To* ROXANE]
He's killed himself, Madame,
In coming here.

ROXANE. Mon dieu!—that faintness, then,
A moment since, was ——

CYRANO. True—I haven't finished
My gazette. On Saturday, an hour
After sunset, Monsieur de Bergerac
Was murdered. [*He takes off his hat.*]

ROXANE. What does he mean?
[*Sees his head bandaged.*]
Cyrano!
What have they done to you?

CYRANO. "Let me die
By the sword of a hero"—that is what I said.
How fate loves a jest! For here I am,
Struck from behind by a hireling with a log
Of wood. I've failed in all things—e'en in death.

RAGUENEAU. [*Falls on his knees, weeping*] Monsieur de Bergerac ——

CYRANO. Stop blubbering, friend.
What are you doing now, my fellow poet?

RAGUENEAU. I—snuff the candles for Molière.

CYRANO. Molière?

RAGUENEAU. I leave to-morrow ——

CYRANO. Leave?

RAGUENEAU. He stole your scene
From Scapin ——

LE BRET. The whole scene?

RAGUENEAU. [*Nods*] They laughed and laughed.

CYRANO.
It is my fate—to prompt and be forgotten.
I spoke for Christian 'neath your balcony:
So have I done in all things all my life—

(*Lights in chapel are lighted at chime cue, and shine out through stained glass windows. These remain lighted to the end.*)

While I stood hidden in darkness down below,
Others climbed to kisses and to fame,
And justly—for on the threshold of the tomb,
I own Molière had genius—Christian, good looks.
[*The Chapel chimes begin to ring and nuns pass, going to vespers.*]

(*Chimes on upper Pin Rail.*)

They are going to pray now. There's the bell!

ROXANE. Sister—Sister ——

CYRANO. No—do not go, Roxane:
When you return, I shall have gone away.
[*An organ is heard from within the chapel. The choir sings softly a short hymn.*]

(*Organ and Choir,* L., *backstage.*)

A little harmony is all I need.

ROXANE. You shall not die—I love you. Stay with me.

CYRANO.
No.—The fairy tale runs differently.

When Beauty said, " I love you," to the Beast,
His ugliness dissolved like snow before
The magic of the sun; but you perceive
That I remain the same.

(*Organ Postlude very softly.*)

ROXANE. And I have done
All this to you.

CYRANO. No—quite the contrary:
Womanhood, with all its sweetness, I
Had never known except for you. My mother
Did not find me good to look upon;
I never had a sister.—Later, I feared
The mistress with the mocking eyes. In you
I've had at least one friend among the fair,
And thanks to you, across my life has passed
The softness of a woman's silken gown.

(*Gradually bring up Blue Spot on* CYRANO'S *chair* R.)

LE BRET. [*Pointing to the moon*] There comes your other friend to see you.

CYRANO. Yes ——

ROXANE. I never loved but one man in my life,
And lost him twice.

CYRANO. Le Bret, I'm going to
The moon.

ROXANE. What did you say?

CYRANO. There—the moon—
My paradise—where I shall find my friends,
Socrates, Galileo ——

LE BRET. 'Tis too absurd—
No.—Such a poet! Such a noble heart—
To die this way.

CYRANO. Hear Le Bret grumble.

LE BRET. [*Bursting into tears*] My friend ——

CYRANO. [*Rising, his eyes wandering*]
We are the Cadets of Gascony—
The elemental mass—yes?

ROXANE. Oh ——

CYRANO. Copernicus said ——

ROXANE. Oh ——

CYRANO. What did he there?
What the devil is he doing there?
Here lies Hercule Savinien
De Cyrano de Bergerac,
Philosopher, physician,
Poet, duellist, musician,
A wit—a lover he—who won no love—
All things he was—but all in vain.
But pardon, I must go—I must not wait;
My moonbeams come to carry me away.

[*Falls back in his chair.* ROXANE'S *sobbing brings him back to reality. He looks at her and caresses her veil.*]

I would not have you shed one tear the less
For Christian, who was so charming and so brave;
I only ask you this; when the great cold
Shall gather round my bones—that for a little
Your widow's veil may have a double meaning,
And in your heart so filled with grief for him
There may sometimes be thoughts of me; sometimes
The tears you shed for him may be my tears.

ROXANE. I swear it ——

CYRANO. [*Shaking as if with cold, suddenly rises*]
No—not here—not in a chair—

Let no one help me—[*leans against tree*] only the tree.
He comes—I feel already shod with stone
And gloved with lead—but since he's on the way,
I'll meet him standing upright—[*draws sword*] sword in hand.

LE BRET. Cyrano ——

ROXANE. Cyrano ——

[*All draw back in terror.*]

CYRANO. He sees my nose!
Well, let the flatnose look me in the face.— [*Raises sword.*]
You say 'tis useless? Very well—I know;
And I have never fought merely to win—
To fight and know one fights in vain is finer—
Who are you all?—A thousand strong.—Ah—now
I know.—You are my ancient enemies;
Falsehood—[*strikes*] there—there—ha, ha; and Compromise,
Prejudice, Cowardice —— Surrender?—No!
Never!—Vanity—you, too;—I knew
That you would lay me low at last. No matter;
While I yet have strength, I'll fight—I'll fight.
[*Swings his sword in circles, then stops.*]
You have snatched them all away—my laurels
And my roses. One thing alone remains
In spite of you, and to-night when on the broad
Blue threshold of God's house I bow before
His throne in low salute—one thing I'll have
Which I have kept unspotted—undefiled—
And that is —— [*He staggers and drops into the arms of* RAGUENEAU *and* LE BRET.]

ROXANE. And that is ——
CYRANO. My white plume.

CURTAIN

CYRANO DE BERGERAC

ACT I.

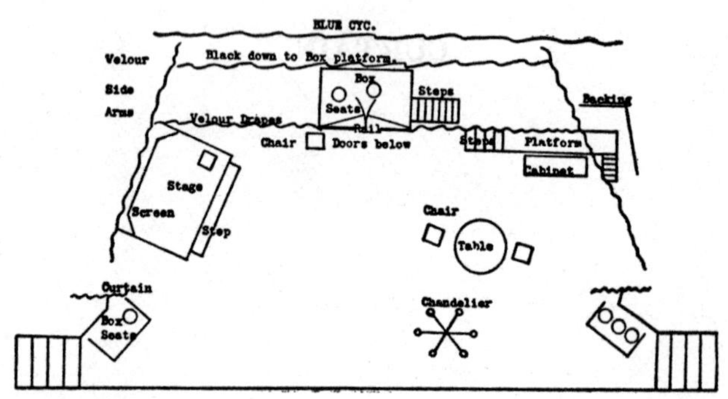

CYRANO DE BERGERAC

ACT II.

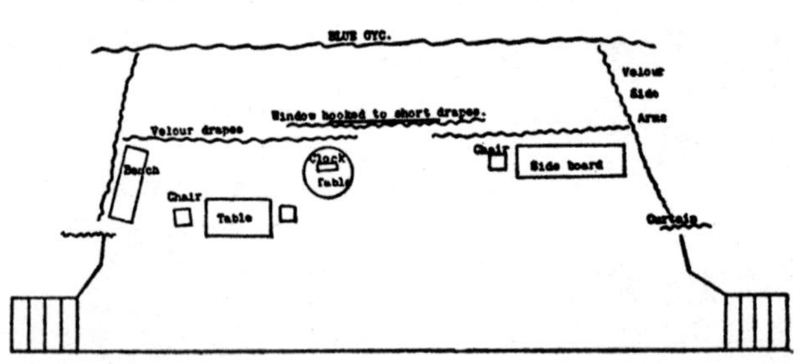

CYRANO DE BERGERAC

ACT III.

BLUE CYC.

Portable Footlights

Velour Side Arms

Velour drapes

Backing

Step ladder

Door

Balcony

Vines & ladder

Rail

Bench

Street lamp

Backing

Platform

Steps

Curtain

CYRANO DE BERGERAC

ACT IV.

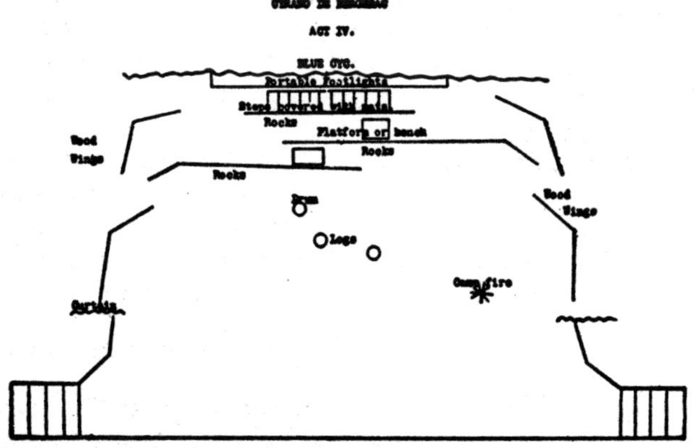

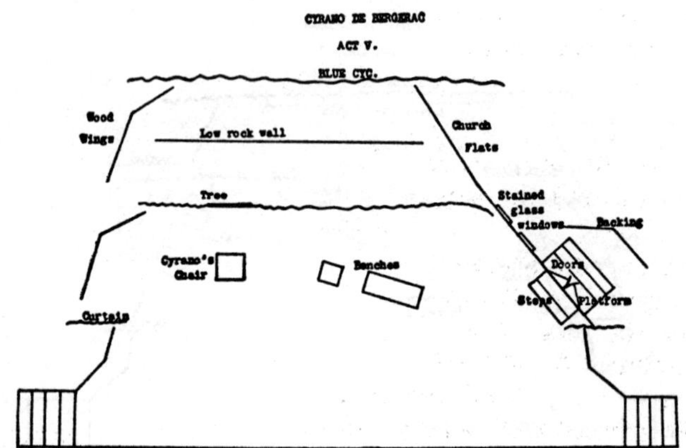
CYRANO DE BERGERAC
ACT V.
BLUE CYC.
Wood
Wings
Low rock wall
Church
Flats
Tree
Stained
glass
windows
Backing
Cyrano's
Chair
Benches
Doors
Steps
Platform
Curtain

PROPERTIES

Act I

Flowers and flower tray.
Tapestry.
Poster, " La Clorise."
Tray and mugs.
Pea shooters.
Lantern.
Cane.
Goblet and other bottles.
Water.
Fruit (grapes, oranges, etc.).
Macaroons and cream puffs.

Act II

Half a dozen hats on a sword.
Large chair.
Paper, quill pen, envelope, inkstand.
Wine cask.
Mugs and pitcher.
Feather duster.
Wine glasses.
Brass plates and rolls.

Act III

Masks.
Lantern.
Street lamp.
Guitar.

Bench (stone).
Three scrolls.
Letter, sealed.
Vines for balcony.

ACT IV

Camp fire.
Logs.
Drum.
Small book.
Letter.
Hamper with food and wine.
Lance.
White scarf.
Lace handkerchief.

ACT V

Large chair.
Soiled letter.
Two stone benches (or one bench and one square stool).
Cane.
Prayer books.
Chimes.
Organ.